KISS A VILLAIN

MIA DARLING

KISS A VILLAIN

NO MERCY DUET
BOOK ONE

MIA DARLING

Once upon a time, I saved a boy from certain death.

Fell for him so hard that I'd follow him straight to the gates of Hell, and say thank you for it.

But the problem with being hopelessly in love with Kirill Volkov is that *he won't ever love me back.*

On paper, we shouldn't even be friends. He's the grump to my sunshine, and he hates to be touched while I'm touch-starved. **Most of all, I'm the prince to a mafia kingdom and he's one of my father's soldiers.**

And everyone knows that the Russian Bratva is a graveyard where all good things go to die.

Day by day, the Kirill I love slips further and further away. Now, when I look in his midnight-black eyes, only a stone-cold killer stares back.

That's okay, though. **There isn't anything I won't do to make him mine...**

Even if it means that I'll need to kiss a villain.

Kiss A Villain (No Mercy Duet, Book 1)

Copyright © 2024 by Mia Darling

All rights reserved.

No part of this book may be reproduced in any form or by any electronic or mechanical means, including information storage and retrieval systems, without written permission from the author, except for the use of brief quotations in a book review.

Cover Artist & Designer: Qamber Designs

Editor: Indie Editing Chick

Beta Readers: Tiana (@aliterarygoddess) & Maya Jean (@mayajeanwrites)

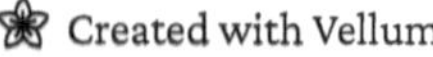 Created with Vellum

To first loves—
To the way they make us bleed.
To the way they make us hurt.
Most of all, to the way they fill us with nothing but hope...

PLAYLIST

Nothing More - "If It Doesn't Hurt"
NF ft. Britt Nicole - "Can You Hold Me"
Tommee Profitt ft. Brooke - "Can't Help Falling In Love"
(DARK)
margø - "guts"
Catch Your Breath - "Dial Tone"
Alan Walker - "Who I Am"
Jutes - Obsessed
Zack Hemsey - "See What I've Become"
Nathan Wagner - "Guilt"
Sleep Token - "Chokehold"
Jim Yosef & Rory Hope - "Risk It All"

To listen to the playlist on Spotify, check out the QR code
below or visit miadarlingbooks.com/playlists

AUTHOR'S NOTE

Yarik & Kirill grow up in the mafia. It is violent, and dark, and psychologically damaging. While I've done my best to treat these scenes with care, please note that there are depictions of emotional manipulation as well as violence within these pages.

Additionally, our boys are still in their early years here—they are grappling with self-identity in the same breath that they're being emotionally suffocated in a world that perceives softness to be a weakness. For a full list of content warnings, continue reading below. Lastly, you'll find a Russian Glossary at the back of this book.

Take care of yourself, first and foremost.

xoxo,

Mia

Violence

References of Self-Harm

Homophobia

Emotional Manipulation

Child Abuse

Voyeurism

Cheating (technically our boys are not yet together but I did want to share this anyway!)

PART ONE
LONDON, ENGLAND

CHAPTER ONE

YARIK

It wouldn't be my first time seeing a dead body.

When I was eight years old, I watched my father slit a man's throat. He made me carry an old, rickety chair into the room. Told me to sit nice and still even when the stranger started screaming, started thrashing, trying desperately to work himself free. The handcuffs caging his wrists were an obstacle. So was the fact that we were miles away from another living soul.

There'd been no one to hear his screams.

No one to save him.

"Watch me, *syn*," Father had ordered while he fisted the man's greasy hair, holding him still. The knife clasped in his other hand glinted under the flickering overhead light. "Don't look away, you hear me?"

I'd wanted to turn tail and run. And if not run, then at least cover my ears to quiet the sound of rubber soles squeaking against linoleum as the stranger struggled against the inevitable. But Petr Volkov wasn't the kind of man you disobeyed—not even when you were his only son—so I'd tucked my clammy hands beneath my trembling thighs and *watched*.

Watched blood bead beneath the tip of the blade.

Watched the man's eyes squeeze shut as he begged for mercy.

Watched the way Father showed him none, the knife flicking neatly across the man's throat to silence him forever.

That was two years ago.

So, no, it wasn't my first time seeing a dead body, but it *would* be my first time seeing one that looked so peaceful. I wasn't sure why the thought of that—of someone dead on account of something other than violence—was so alluring, but here I was.

Carefully, I crept through the tall reeds, my footsteps muffled by the distant hum of traffic on the other side of the River Thames. Moonlight spilled across my thin arms as I used a large stick to slash my way through to the riverbank. My cousin Vera had said that the body was here, but Vera was also something of a liar. Last year, she'd convinced me that the Fae were real. Another time, when I was five, she tricked me into thinking that I wasn't a true Volkov, that I'd been snatched from my real family at birth.

"God, you're *glupyy*," she'd sneered after I had burst into tears. "Stupid and *soft*."

Father called me stupid, too, sometimes. Except that I wasn't stupid and I definitely wasn't *soft*, whatever that meant. It was just that my brain worked differently. At least that was what Mama always said before she'd died.

Either way, Father was away on another one of his trips back to Russia which meant that until he came back, *I* was in charge. If there was a dead body on our land, then I'd have to be the one to do something about it.

Ignoring the way my pulse scrambled with nerves, I pushed past the remaining undergrowth and stepped out into the open.

A cool autumn breeze swept around my exposed calves, pebbling my skin with goose bumps. Up ahead, the path disappeared into an endless streak of midnight black. We lived in a big terrace house in London's West End, but whenever Father went out of town, he preferred that me and my little sister, Nina, stay on the family estate instead. Out here, it was easy to feel like the last person on Earth, the darkness so thick that you could choke on it.

A shiver of foreboding slithered down my spine.

Fumbling in my pocket, I pulled out the torch that I'd brought with me and turned it on, angling the harsh yellow light directly ahead of my feet. Dirt. Pebbles. Not much else. Holding in an anxious breath, I swung the light toward my left, then my right, then squared my shoulders and marched onward.

Maybe this was another one of Vera's tricks.

Maybe she was out here, too, just biding her time until she could pop out of the bushes and bust me for being *glupyy*.

Stupid.

Stupid.

Stupid—

I squeezed the torch in an angry fist, hating the thought that maybe she'd gotten the better of me yet again. She'd probably made it all up, too—sat in her bedroom with her fuzzy slippers and a mug of steaming chocolate that she'd ordered Chef to make her even though he'd gotten off the clock hours ago. Vera didn't *ask* anyone for anything.

I *hated* her.

What I hated even more was the fact that my hands were trembling.

I could admit that I was scared, which normally wouldn't be a problem because I was constantly surrounded by Father's soldiers, except that I'd managed to sneak out past the guards, which meant that no one aside from Vera—and maybe my sister Nina—knew where I was. That was a first. For as long as I could remember, Father had assigned two of his best men to be my own personal shadow.

It was so dark out that I couldn't even see *my* shadow.

I swallowed, tightly.

Okay. So what if I was completely alone? And so what if there *was* a dead body around here somewhere? I'd . . . Well, I'd just have to—

I fell.

No, I *tripped*.

The stick went flying from my grasp, the cavernous dark suddenly illuminated by a cone of yellow as the torch landed with a dull thud in the grass. Scrambling to my knees, I snatched it up and twisted around to shine a light on whatever had taken me down.

Dark, red-rimmed eyes peered back at me.

Oh.

Oh, bloody hell.

The body wasn't dead.

I careened backward with a startled yelp, tripping over my feet and falling onto my arse in the dirt. On my descent, the torchlight revealed shattered fragments: a sopping-wet arm reaching for me, torn fabric and a sliver of skin, and then, lastly, the face of a boy not much older than me.

"Wait."

His voice was hoarse, pleading.

Fear kept mine lodged like a blade stuck in my throat.

For a second, we remained like that, me on the verge of running, him splayed out on the packed dirt like a discarded doll. *An afterthought.* It almost hurt to look at him. There was a bloody knot on his temple and more of it seeping from the corner of his lips, which he licked at nervously as if he could tell that it'd caught my attention.

I couldn't bring myself to look away.

Where had he come from?

Slowly, he let his outstretched arm lower to the ground. Light fractured across his knuckles as he dug his fingertips into the hard, unforgiving earth, clearly trying to push himself up into a sitting position. But he didn't— he *couldn't*—

Strength seeped right out of him, and he collapsed.

I crawled to his side on my knees.

Being Petr Volkov's son, I knew just about everyone around here. But I'd never met *him*. I definitely would have remembered.

This close, I could see that dirt and blood caked the side of his face. I lifted my hand without thought, stroking my thumb across his cold cheek to wipe it clean. The boy hissed under my touch, too weak to do anything but jerk his face away.

I pulled back instantly.

"I didn't mean—I-I'm sorry," I stammered. *Stupid. Stupid.* Heat flushed in my cheeks as I lurched to my feet.

Whoever this boy was, he wasn't dead.

That meant he wasn't my problem.

Someone had to be looking for him, right? Maybe it was a good thing Father was away; he didn't like anyone trespassing on his property. The last time it happened, he set the dogs loose. I hadn't seen what happened next, but I always figured it couldn't have been good. Even Vera had kept her mouth shut for the rest of the day.

"You can't stay here," I said. "It's not safe."

He didn't respond.

I turned to look back at him, aiming the torch at the ground beside his limp frame so that the artificial light didn't glare directly in his face. There was even more blood now. It dripped down over his browbone in a steady stream, and the way his damp hair lay across his forehead revealed more blood congealed around his ear.

He really didn't look so good.

"I don't know where you came from." With an audible squelch, the soles of my trainers sank into a patch of mud. "I don't know who you *are*."

No reply.

Nothing but the unsteady rise and fall of his thin chest.

"I should leave you here." Biting my lip, I swung a quick glance over my shoulder, just to check if we were still alone, before drawing to a stop beside him. "Father won't care that you're a kid, barely older than me. He thinks you're trouble, he'll put a bullet in your brain and bury you where no one will ever find you again."

He'd brought me to that cabin.

Slit a man's throat in that cabin and made me watch.

Later, he'd handed me a shovel and told me to dig.

"I don't think you deserve to die like that," I whispered, as though Father could actually hear me, all the way in Moscow. "But I think if I leave you here, you'll die anyway."

Everyone said that I was stupid, and I must be, because instead of doing the smart thing and walking away, I lowered to my haunches and warily eyed the almost dead boy in front of me. I was big for my age. Always had been. For once, my size worked to my benefit because it let me slide an arm under the boy's narrow back. I wouldn't be able to carry him all the way home, but I could at least take on most of his weight.

He whimpered as I dragged him onto his feet and hugged him close to my side. "You'll probably regret this," I said quietly. Then I put one foot in front of the other, already knowing that I was making a grave mistake.

"WHAT THE FUCK, Yarik? You *brought him here?*"

Vera was five years older than me. After her birthday a few months ago, I'd thought turning fifteen might change her a little, but as she stared at me with her jaw practically on the floor, it suddenly seemed pretty obvious that age had nothing to do with the core of a human being. She was still the same snake that she'd always been, and I'd still seen toddlers with more backbone.

"You can't just—" Clearly flustered, her fingers curled around the lip of the door like she wanted to close it in my face. "This isn't a good idea."

"You're the one who told me about him."

"Yeah, but I didn't think you'd *do* anything about it!" I half expected her to stomp her feet, but she just glared at me from under her dark brown fringe, the shade a sharp contrast to my own blond hair. "Besides, I thought he was dead."

"Well, he's not." I was sweating through my clothes. The walk from the river had started to feel like a never-ending nightmare by the time we'd reached the halfway point near the gnarled oak tree with its ancient branches that almost kissed the ground. More than once, the boy's legs had given out beneath him, and more than once, we'd had to stop and rest. Now, I was barely holding him upright, his weight feeling as if it might slip right through my fingers.

"Are you going to help me or not?" I demanded.

My cousin skimmed the both of us with a critical eye. "Not."

"*Idi na hui,*" I growled, elbowing her aside.

"Learning some big words now, are we, *dvoyurodnyy brat?*" She trailed after us, keeping up a running stream of commentary as I tried to stick to the corridors that were designated for the housekeeping staff. "If it were anyone else, I'd say that you're about to get caught, but that's not going to happen, is it? You're so boring that your guards probably think you're asleep in your room right now. I bet they don't even know you left."

I gritted my teeth.

"What are you even going to do with him? Keep him like a pet?"

"He's not a *pet.*"

"You'll have to feed him, won't you?"

Why wouldn't she just *shut up?* "I'm not going to let him starve him, Vera."

"He'll need water, too."

"I know," I snapped.

"So, he needs to be fed and watered. Sounds like a pet to me. Or a plant."

"You're so annoying."

"At least I'm not already dead."

"He's not—"

"I'm not talking about him, Yarik. I'm talking about *you*. You're totally going to die for this, so what's the point of going through all the effort to save him?"

The sad truth was, she wasn't lying. When Father caught wind of this, I'd be lucky if the only thing he did was string me up and whip my back raw. He'd done it before, too. More times than I could count. These days, I knew better than to voice the thoughts inside my head.

Around Petr Volkov, it was safer to say nothing at all.

"Hold on," I muttered to the boy even though I was pretty sure he'd passed out long before we'd reached the house. I was more or less hauling him along, my left arm wrapped around his waist while I clutched his right hand in mine, his arm growing heavier and heavier where it rested across my shoulders. "Just a little bit more."

"Where'd he come from, anyway?" Vera asked.

"I don't know." The better question was, "What were *you* doing down by the river?"

When Vera didn't answer, I turned to find that she'd conveniently disappeared.

Figured.

My cousin would happily interrogate someone for hours but rarely sat in the hot seat herself.

I was panting by the time we made it to my room. It took some awkward shuffling to get the door open, but I managed well enough until we were safely tucked away behind the closed door—no lock, unfortunately. Father wouldn't allow us any—and I had him laid out on my bed.

He looked like a fallen angel.

"Just . . . just stay there." Clumsily, I fluffed the pillow behind his head like that was the worst of his problems. "I'll be right back."

Then I darted into the loo, where I pushed aside a small cabinet before dropping down onto my knees. If Father knew that I'd taken a hammer to his wall—or that I'd made a habit of sneaking into Uncle Igor's medical room, to forage for a makeshift First Aid kit—he'd go berserk. Punishments, he always said, were meant to be endured like a man.

If he took a lash to my skin, I wasn't allowed to cry.

If he made me bleed, I was meant to stoically withstand the pain.

I was his heir, the prince to his criminal empire, and he'd kill me himself before he ever let me be a disappointment to the Volkov name.

So maybe I was boring like Vera said, but being boring definitely had its perks. Mainly, being able to move around as I wanted without attracting attention from my bodyguards. Contrary to what everyone thought of me, I'd grown to appreciate living in the shadows. It was the only time I ever felt free.

With the contraband cradled in my arms, I hightailed it back to the bed. He hadn't moved at all, hands limp on his stomach, legs still casually draped over the side of the mattress where I'd left them.

He seemed so . . . *lifeless.*

I wasn't the one who'd left him out there to die, but I couldn't help feeling strangely guilty as I looked down at him. "I'm sorry this happened to you."

I'm even sorrier that you're stuck with me.

Didn't matter that I'd never tended to anyone but myself before; I was all he had. Plus, if I'd figured out how to stitch up my own injuries, then I could certainly fix *him*.

Squaring my shoulders, I dumped my stash on the bedside table. There were a few things I was running low on, but I wasn't willing to risk venturing into Uncle Igor's wing of the mansion, not so soon after he'd been forced to stay behind while Father traveled without him. Sometimes, Father did that—played mental games with his younger brother so Uncle Igor rarely ever dropped his guard. He couldn't, not when every aspect of his life sat clutched in the palm of a predator.

Luckily, I'd stuck to the shadows well enough over the years, quietly watching Uncle Igor as he patched up Father's soldiers, so I had a decent understanding of what needed to be done. Cleansing wipes. Antibacterial cream. I grabbed both to start with, sat my arse down on the corner of the mattress, and got to work.

It was the first time I was able to really *look* at him.

He was of Asian descent with olive skin, an angular face, and hair black like a raven's. With a pang of empathy, I went to push the matted strands off his forehead before yanking my hand back just as quickly. He hadn't appreciated being touched. Chewing my bottom lip, I swept my gaze over the rest of him. I'd been right about his age; he couldn't be any older than eleven or twelve. With his eyes closed like they were, he looked even younger. The strained furrow between his brows had faded, and so had the tension pinching his mouth. His still-damp clothes were dirty with dried blood and whatever else lurked at the bottom of the River Thames.

On a second pass, I noticed bruises on the backs of his hands.

What happened to you?

While I cleaned him up, I couldn't help but let my brain run wild. Maybe he'd slipped in by accident and had been caught in the current. Or maybe he'd been pushed—in my world, that was more likely—and he'd never stood a chance.

However he'd ended up like this, I couldn't keep him here forever. Sooner or later, we'd be found out.

The minutes passed by in silence as I bent over him, carefully cleaning and then closing the gash on his temple with tiny little stitches. It was a lot easier to work on someone else for a change, and when I finished, I sat back with a giddy rush of pride. Those stitches were perfect. Better than any I'd ever done. It wasn't like Uncle Igor or Father were here to see them, and it wasn't as if I'd show them even if they were, but that didn't stop me from wanting to scream, *See? I'm not stupid like you all think I am.*

"I know it probably doesn't feel like it right now," I said to the boy, watching his face closely for any sign of acknowledgment before I turned to put my things away, "but you're totally going to live. We'll have to figure out how to get you out of here when you wake up, though, so don't start thinking that you're in the clear."

He didn't say anything, but that was okay.

I'd *saved* him.

HIS SKIN WAS HOT.

I rushed to the bathroom and grabbed hand towels from the drawer beneath the sink, turning the cold tap on in a hurry before shoving the whole bundle under the lukewarm water.

Colder, I needed it to be *colder*.

Just to spite me, the water stayed lukewarm.

From the bedroom, I heard a small moan of discomfort. He'd started kicking at the sheets an hour ago. At first, I thought maybe he was having a nightmare, but even after kicking almost all of the blankets to the foot of the bed, he'd been unable to stay still. Now he was burning up, and *why wouldn't the water get any colder?*

Unwilling to wait another second, I left the tap running as I sprinted back to my room, where I kneeled at his side, panic gripping my lungs. "I'm going to fix you. I promise, okay? Just . . ." With a damp hand, I grabbed the single sheet tangled around his calf and flung it to the floor. "We just need to cool you off, that's all."

That's all.

As I pressed one of the lukewarm towels to his feverish skin, I squeezed my eyes shut and did the one thing that I hadn't since we'd lost Mama—I prayed.

Please don't let him die.

Please tell me that I didn't kill him.

Please, please, please.

"I don't know—I'm sorry—"

The wet towels weren't working. Cleaning his wounds hadn't helped. My hands trembled so much that I dropped the pill bottle twice before I managed to crack the top open and shake one out into my sweaty palm.

I looked down at the pill. I looked up at the boy.

"I don't know how to help you." My voice quivered with the admission. I was terrified, and he was deathly hot, and I was in over my head. If I waited any longer, he might die. If I sought out help, they might kill him. It felt like my back was up against a wall and there was no way out. I was running out of time—

The boy let out a cry.

The tortured sound rose the hair on my nape, and I stumbled toward him with the pill still clutched in my clammy fist. "Hold on," I begged him, my gaze moving frantically over thrashing limbs. "Please, just hold on—"

SHADOWS CLUNG to every corner of Uncle Igor's wing.

For once, I wished Vera was still tailing me, if only so her constant chatter would put an end to the ominous silence that permeated this side of the mansion. But she wasn't here, and it was just me, so I forced one foot in front of the other, knowing with every step I took that if I liked having my head attached to my shoulders, I should turn my arse around and never look back.

No one really needed to know about the boy.

You can always hide his body after.

Thanks to Father's many lessons, I was good at that—getting rid of the evidence—so what was I doing, stopping in front of Uncle Igor's bedroom door when I knew that he preferred to be left alone? Forget that—why was I even lifting a fist to knock on the dark wood?

Run.

My ears pricked at the squeal of mattress springs followed immediately by the heavy tread of footsteps.

Run.

There was a small pause as if he was deliberately gathering his hard-fought patience, before the knob jiggled, turned.

Run.

The door swung open, and cold blue eyes peered down at me from a face carved by the hand of fire, the old, twisted scars alongside his temple and cheek appearing even more sinister in the dim lighting. Uncle Igor propped a hand on the doorframe, his big body looming over mine.

"What do you want?"

I opened my mouth to reply, and, to my horror, nothing came out.

Disgust flitted across his weathered face. "Let's try that again." He didn't wait for me to speak. "What can I do for you?"

Every molecule in my body itched to flee. This was a bad idea. All of it. I should have left the boy by the river. Should have ignored Vera in the first place when she mentioned seeing a dead body. None of it was my business, and what was I even thinking, trying to save him?

Stupid.

Stupid.

Stu—

"Yaroslav."

"I n-need . . ." Fear crowded my heart, and the whole corridor seemed to tilt sideways. It was too late now. I could run with my tail tucked between my legs or voice exactly what I'd come here to say—I'd suffer the same fate either way. More lashes. More scars. I scraped together the fragments of my courage, trembling fists locked together at the base of my spine, out of sight from prying eyes, and confessed:

"I-I think I k-killed him."

CHAPTER TWO

YARIK

"Do you have anything to say for yourself?"

"I'm sorry, Papa. I . . . I didn't mean for your trip to be cut short."

"Did you think that I wouldn't find out? That your uncle wouldn't phone me?"

"N-no."

"No, *what*?"

"No, *Otets*."

"Get the rope."

I'd predicted this outcome the moment I slung my arm around the boy's waist and half-carried him to shelter. Because this property *would* shelter him, even if that shelter came with conditions, and even if that shelter functioned as my very own prison.

Angry, resentful tears burned behind my eyelids as I slowly reached up and gathered the coiled length of rope from where it hung on the wall in my father's study. Its weight was horribly familiar. I knew, intimately, how each fiber chafed my skin raw. When I was younger, I pushed back however I could—biting, clawing, kicking—

until Father taught me a lesson that left me unable to speak for weeks. It was hard to accept his punishments, but it was even harder knowing that if I fought back in any way, I would live to regret it.

Wordlessly, I pressed the rope into my father's waiting hand.

"Wrists," he demanded, voice still deceptively calm.

I held them out.

He cinched the rope tight enough to stem the flow of circulation, forcing my palms together in a mockery of prayer. Or maybe it wasn't a mockery at all; as he ordered me to loop my bound wrists over the same hook that had held the rope, I couldn't help but feel as if it was God at my back, punishing me for simply breathing.

The first lash across my bare back made me cry out.

The second lifted me onto my toes in a desperate bid to squirm away.

The third came.

Then the fourth and the fifth.

By the tenth, there were no more tears or panicked breaths. I simply existed, a broken boy who craved the shadows, where nothing and no one could hurt him.

CHAPTER THREE

"*ey*. Hey, wake up."

What felt like a small finger poked me in the side. Paralyzing fear followed right after, bleeding through my consciousness as I went taut like a stretched elastic band.

"Oh, come on," that same voice whined. "I *know* you can hear me. The doctor said he stopped with the mor . . . *mar*feen, or whatever it's called, so why are you pretending to be asleep?"

Before I could react, a weight suddenly collapsed beside me. It was so unexpected that my eyes flew open, only to find a girl perched on her knees near my hip, her pale white hands clutching her thighs like that was the only thing holding her back. The air practically vibrated around her, her eagerness—for what, I wasn't sure— grossly palpable.

I didn't recognize her.

My gaze flew past her blond head, searching the room we were in for something familiar. The walls were bare with a single window overlooking a murky gray sky.

There was a desk, too, but it was too far away for me to get a good look at the papers stacked on top of it.

The girl's stare followed the direction mine had strayed. "Do you want me to get them for you?" she asked, cocking her head in a way that instantly put me on alert.

I didn't say anything back.

Couldn't, honestly, because there was a panicked lump growing in my throat.

Who was she?

Where was I?

"Do you understand what I'm saying?" Her tone was curious. "If you can't, I speak Russian, too." She tilted her head even more, the long length of her white-blond hair hanging like a veil in front of her narrow face. "Do you speak Russian?" She launched into a string of foreign-sounding words that barely penetrated the thick fog swirling around my brain.

The more she talked, the more animated she became and the closer she got to me.

Stop, I wanted to shout.

Get back.

Then her knee pressed into my thigh, her hand moving to my shin, and the elastic band snapped; I jerked away so violently that the sheet wrapped around my legs went tight for one wretched second before loosening completely and dumping me on the floor in an ungraceful heap. Pain erupted in a flash of heat across my body, but I almost didn't care how badly I hurt.

I just needed space—to breathe, to think.

Where was I?

Who was she?

Don't touch me.

There was a sudden commotion behind me, a door cracking open, a sharply uttered, "Nina, I told you to stay out of this room," but all of it was muffled because, at some point, I'd curled into a ball on the floor, hands pressed against my ringing ears, one loose thread away from opening my mouth on a bloodcurdling scream.

Who was she?

Where was I?

Don't touch—

"Boy." This belonged to a deep, thickly accented voice. "Calm yourself."

A hand landed on my shoulder. It was heavier than the girl's, the weight of it like an anchor, yanking me straight down to the ocean floor. Maybe he thought the casual touch would ground me, but it had the opposite effect, spiking my already shallow breathing to the point where I gasped for air.

Frozen in place, I didn't pull my hands away from my ears even as he continued to stare at me as if I was already a lost cause. Just like with the girl, I didn't recognize him either.

"You were found almost dead by the river," he said without preamble. "Do you remember?"

Almost dead . . .

A violent shiver whispered down my spine. I didn't remember a river, and I didn't remember being almost dead. Then I actually took a moment to look down at myself and realized that in my tumble to the floor, I'd ripped an IV out from the back of my hand. There were bruises. Like I'd fought something and lost. A hasty, upward glance revealed that behind the . . . the hospital bed, it looked like, there was a bunch of medical equipment that hadn't been in view before. And I was wearing some sort of paper-thin gown, like the kind patients wore in hospital.

"The doctor said you're lucky that you weren't out there all night."

I didn't feel lucky. I felt like I'd been hit by a lorry gunning at full speed. Despite the throbbing pain radiating from my temple, there was no ignoring the mammoth-sized man in front of me. He had a stocky build with a thick neck, along with dark brown hair that had been combed back from his face with ruthless precision. He looked like a villain in a fairy tale, the one who locked the princess in the tower or fed her poison apples.

"Take your hands off your ears."

It was self-preservation alone that made me do it, just to avoid the possibility of being beaten to a bloody pulp.

As my whole body recoiled from the sheer size of his, he said, "Who sent you?"

I shook my head because I didn't know what that meant—who *sent* me—but the hand on my shoulder moved to grasp my upper arm, so that I had no choice but to sit right there in front of him, still half-curled into myself, while he followed up with, "I don't believe in coincidences, so I'll ask one more time: *Who sent you?*"

I didn't have an answer for him.

"Was it Kurobara?" His gaze hardened. "Cadwell?"

Why those names?

Did he know me? Know *them*?

The grip on my arm tightened. Under different circumstances, the pressure might have been insubstantial, but if I had to guess, he was pressing down on another unanswered-for bruise, which meant that it *hurt*. I let out a hiss, retreating with a backward scramble that put me under the elevated hospital bed, where I hunched over to keep from hitting the top of my head. With my pulse beating out of control, I felt almost feral, wanting to run but not knowing where to go.

The door was shut.

The girl was gone.

"What's your name?" the man asked almost kindly, clearly changing tactics. When I only stared back, giving him nothing, the last of his patience seemed to chip away. "The thing about rescuing an almost dead boy is that I can't tell you the story that came before—maybe you slipped away from your family, entirely by accident, or maybe you ran away because that was your only option. Do you see my dilemma?" He spread his big hands wide, the gesture as harmless as an emaciated lion bedded down with a herd of gazelles. "I don't know whether to return you to your family or keep you safe."

This didn't feel safe.

My heart was racing, and the hairs on my nape stood on end. Despite every gut instinct screaming that I couldn't trust him, or this place, I heard myself rasp, "Who are . . . they?"

"Cadwell and Kurobara?"

Something in his tone told me that there was history there. A reason why he doubted my innocence. Like he thought that I was some kind of Trojan horse, washed up on his land to make his life a living hell. But he was wrong. Throat tight, I gave a quick jerk of my head. No, I didn't know them. I didn't know any of these people.

"Do you know your name?" he asked again.

The question rattled around in my skull, knocking emotions loose even though no memories shook out.

Didn't I have a name? Everyone had a name.

Straining for an answer only worsened the high-pitched ringing in my ears, so I dug my thumbs into my temple, praying that everything would just go *quiet*. It didn't, because of course it didn't. Nausea swirled in my belly like a bad omen.

"You don't remember anything?"

"A boy," I heard myself say before I even realized that I'd opened my mouth. "I remember . . . a boy."

I didn't remember his face or his name, if he'd even given it to me, but I remembered the sensation of being shored up against a lanky frame, of a soft, lulling voice speaking quietly in my ear, of falling to the ground and there never being any loss of patience—just quiet understanding until his arm was back around my waist and mine once again grasped desperately onto him, and then . . . nothing.

Blank space.

The stranger stared at me. I couldn't read his thoughts, his gaze was that impenetrable, but then his mouth sort of pinched, and he slowly rose to his full height. From where I hid, I couldn't see anything above his belt buckle, so I watched his shiny shoes as they took him away.

Was he leaving?

What did he plan to do with—

"Get me Yarik." The order was given without fanfare to whoever waited in the hall. Then he stood sentry at the door, the questioning he'd put forth lapsing into awkward silence.

I glanced from his legs to the base of the window. I didn't know what floor we were on, and I didn't know how extensive my injuries were from being *almost dead*, but I knew that this place felt off, this stranger felt off, and whether or not he actually planned to keep me safe —all of this felt *off*.

"I wouldn't do that if I were you."

I'd barely gotten one palm on the tiled floor. Technically, I hadn't *done* anything. But I heard the subtle edge in his voice and went absolutely still, instinctively knowing better than to aggravate the emaciated lion.

His impatience permeated the air.

"Here, on this land, everything belongs to me. This house, these trees, the fucking air you breathe. If I let you stay, it's because I have a use for you. If I let you go, I won't be hunting down your family to give you some happy little reunion. I'll drop you off at the edge of my land, where you can't breathe my fucking air, and I'll send you on your way. Do we understand each other?"

Not safe.

The warning clanged like a bell in my head.

I eyed the window again, debating how far I could get before the stranger took me out—because he would, I knew that now—but then the door cracked open, and a new pair of shoes entered my periphery. These legs were shorter, thinner, the trainers worn with age, the once-white laces now an obscure shade of gray, like the sky beyond the window, like the feeling running rampant in my chest.

Gray like defeat.

Gray like hopelessness.

"Papa, Pavel said you wanted to see me."

That voice.

I found myself peeking out from under the bed, just to put a face to my only memory. *Thin arms holding me up; "You can't stay here—it's not safe," whispered fervently in my ear.*

He looked nothing at all like I'd expected.

The voice was soft, even now when addressing his father, but the rest of him spoke of an inner strength that bled through to the surface. His chin was tipped down toward his chest, not in subservience but in quiet revolt —it was there in the way a muscle ticked in his jaw, in the way his fingers furled and unfurled where he kept them laced together at the base of his spine, out of his father's sight. His blond hair was nearly as white as the girl's from earlier—siblings, if I had to guess—and the wavy strands fell across a pair of dark blue eyes that glittered with defiance even as he kept them trained on the floor.

"Is this the boy you remember?" the stranger said.

That's when those blue eyes lifted and found me in my hiding place, tucked away under the bed like a coward. Mortification burned in my cheeks as I scrabbled out, my right knee almost slipping out from under me as I pitched awkwardly to my feet.

I was strangely nervous as I met his gaze. Utterly breathless when I said, "You saved me."

"He almost killed you," the stranger scoffed cruelly. And then he clasped his son's nape the way a bitch would to a newborn pup. Only, the boy—Yarik?—didn't immediately go pliant under his father's touch. No, he bristled and bared his teeth, and then the stranger seemed to realize that he had a rebellion on his hands because he shifted his grip downward. Tears suddenly glistened in those dark blue eyes, that lanky frame nearly curling into itself as a choked-off whimper escaped his parted lips.

Something about that—watching all that defiance be snuffed out like a dampened candle wick—made a rush of emotion flood my veins. I didn't recognize it. Didn't even understand it. None of that stopped me.

I discovered a small limp on my second step across the room.

On my third, I realized that the ties on my hospital gown had loosened. The thin material gaped in the back as cool air rushed over my skin, bare arse and all. That didn't stop me either.

I walked right up to Yarik as if our meeting had always been inevitable. He was taller than me. Broader, too. This close, it was easy to see that his skin wasn't nearly as flawless as it had looked from across the room; freckles spilled across the bridge of his nose and cheekbones. His face was soft in a way that said, one day, when he grew even taller and his body became a junkyard of hardened memories, each of his boyish features would die a quick and brutal death. He had a warrior's heart. I knew it even though I wasn't sure how.

If his father was the villain in a fairy tale, then this boy was the prince.

I wasn't sure what that made me. An interloper, maybe. The cast-off character with a single memorable line but who is otherwise destined to be forgotten.

Guess I'd better make it count, then.

In the span of a single heartbeat, I wrapped myself around Yarik's rangy body—one arm looped behind his warm neck, the other anchored around his waist, my hands pressed flat against his spine. Even as I held him to me, I heard the way my breathing hitched under a sudden onslaught of panic. I wanted to rip myself out of his arms, wanted to scrub every last place on my body that now carried the memory of his touch. It took every ounce of willpower to keep still.

Could he feel how my heart raced?

Did he even realize that my little maneuver had forced his father to let go?

I met the stranger's gaze over Yarik's shoulder. They both had the same dark blue eyes, and I didn't dare look away, not even when I opened my mouth and murmured against the shell of Yarik's ear, "Thank you. Thank you for saving me."

"I couldn't leave you." The son's quiet admission sparked a wildfire in the father's eyes. "Not like that."

Before I could respond, Yarik was torn from my hold, the unforgiving grip on the back of his neck forcing his head down as the stranger towed him toward the door, where he was pushed into the hallway. Then the stranger turned back toward me, the irritation in his expression barely leashed by a mask of civility.

I was the *almost-dead* boy. The boy who'd been dredged from the Thames and saved by a single stroke of luck. There was terror crawling through my veins, sure, but also something that felt suspiciously like dumb bravado. Which had to be the only reason I looked the stranger dead in the eye and said, "Do you feel better about yourself when you push your son around?"

The mask fell away.

In its place was raw, unrelenting fury.

He took a menacing step toward me. "You have until the end of the day. If I find you still on my land—"

"Breathing your fucking air," I interjected, throwing his own words back at him, just to see how that fury glimmered.

"—You'll wish that you'd died in that fucking river."

And then he was gone.

I glanced at the window and wondered how far the fall was.

CHAPTER FOUR

The stranger's name was Petr Volkov.

I learned it the same day as that first meeting, not long after he spotted me limping along the side of the road and pulled his posh car over. I thought maybe he'd come to finish me off. Wouldn't have been hard, really, what with how bad I felt, but he'd only put down the passenger window and said, "Get in."

That was it. Get in.

Worst part was, I'd *done* it.

All it took was one long look at the unfamiliar road stretched out before me and I'd climbed into the passenger seat without a backward glance. Maybe because I had nowhere else to go. Because my head throbbed and every part of my body ached, and I wore a hospital gown like a shawl to keep the chill out of my bones. Either way, as I'd stood there while a gust of wind whipped off the scraggly tree limbs overhead, I'd decided that it was better to stick with the devil I knew than the one I didn't.

Or maybe that was a whole crock of shit.

Pretty sure Petr Volkov knew it, too.

I spent that day, and every one that followed, being interrogated:

"What do you remember from before the river?" *Nothing.*

"Nothing? How do you remember *nothing?*" *How do you know the sky is blue? I don't remember anything. If I did, I'd tell you.*

"I don't think you would." A small shrug. *That's your problem then, not mine.*

"It's *your* problem, too, boy, if I think you know more than you're letting on." *The only thing I know is that I haven't seen Yarik. Where is he?*

As the weeks wore on, invoking Yarik's name became my get-out-of-jail-free card. Mention Volkov's son and it was game over immediately. One minute, I'd be stuck at a table while Petr cleaned a gun, a blade, some random kitchen knife that he plucked from a drawer, and in the next, I was set loose on the estate, allowed to wander wherever I wanted even though I knew that there were eyes on me at all times.

It was a fabricated sort of freedom.

I'd given up any chance at the real kind the moment that I panicked on the side of an empty road and chose to stay with the devil instead.

Early on, I met Igor Volkov and his daughter, Vera. Yarik's little sister Nina became my personal shadow, following me everywhere, peppering me with questions that I didn't know the answer to, speaking in Russian whenever my silence annoyed her—which was often. It didn't take a genius to figure out that the Volkovs weren't exactly living on the straight and narrow. There were bodyguards assigned to every member of the family, not to mention the fact that Petr kept odd hours, often rushing off in the dead of night or holding meetings in his study just as late.

They put me up in a room that overlooked the front drive. Besides having a place to hide from Nina, it meant that I could watch the comings and goings of the house.

It meant that I could watch for *Yarik*.

His disappearance didn't make any sense. Petr Volkov was a mean bastard all right, but I didn't think he'd off his own son. Maim or injure, maybe, but kill? Too messy. Volkov struck me as the sort of person who liked things neat and orderly even when he was the one orchestrating chaos.

Whenever I wasn't required to sit for another one of his inquisitions, I roamed the mansion's endless hallways in search of his son, peeking behind closed doors and never getting much of anywhere.

And then one day, I opened a door and found him unpacking a suitcase.

I must have made a noise of surprise because his head jerked up and his eyes went comically wide. A second later, his freckled cheeks flushed a brilliant red, and he practically slammed the luggage shut before darting in front of the bed to block the contents with his body.

Unsure of my welcome, I lingered on the threshold. "What are you hiding?"

It wasn't hello.

It wasn't even, *You're probably wondering why I'm still in your house.*

It was rude and audacious, and I felt my own cheeks burn.

I opened my mouth to apologize, but Yarik had already squared off his hips for a fight. "What makes you think I'm hiding anything?"

"You couldn't close the suitcase fast enough."

"Maybe it's a secret."

"I'm pretty sure you don't get to keep secrets in a house like this." A week ago, I'd found what looked like an armory behind one of the mansion's many closed doors. I had a feeling the only one who successfully kept secrets around here was Petr Volkov and maybe his brother, Igor. Not for the first time, it made me wonder if I was about to become another Volkov secret.

I still didn't understand why Petr had changed his mind about me.

Then again, maybe he hadn't. Maybe I was going to go to bed one night and just never wake up, and then I'd never have the chance to tell the man to go fuck himself.

Feeling a little bold, I stepped into the bedroom, watching avidly as Yarik slung himself up onto the tall, four-poster bed so he could sit cross-legged on top of the suitcase like a bird sat on its nest or a dragon guarding a horde of treasure. He dropped his hands onto his thighs and studied me with that defiant blue gaze.

"I have loads of secrets," he announced.

"Like what?"

He didn't answer right away, but strangely, a reply felt unnecessary. The way he'd disappeared after that first day, how he spoke openly with me now as if he was totally unsurprised to find me in his room, told me that he'd known all along that I was living on the property.

Suddenly, I didn't feel all that brave.

I felt thrown off-balance, like the night I'd almost

drowned. Ears ringing, throat tight, aches and bruises throbbing like invisible wounds beneath my skin.

"Your father picked me up on the side of the road when I tried to leave," I heard myself say.

"I know."

"He interrogates me every day. From the moment I wake up until whenever I annoy him enough that he lets me go. And then he does it again twenty-four hours later."

Yarik's gaze didn't waver. "I know."

"He thinks I'm a . . . a *spy* or something, doesn't he?"

No answer.

"Cadwell. Kurobara. Who are they?"

Still nothing.

I nearly exploded with frustration. "How does your father know them? Why does he think *they* know *me*? Please," I said in a rush, "you have to tell me *something*."

Biting his bottom lip, Yarik darted his gaze away. Just when I thought he'd avoid yet another one of my questions, he spoke in a too-careful voice that had me straightening my shoulders because this—whatever this was—had to be important.

"Their names are Ian Cadwell and Kage Kurobara. My father . . ."

"Your father, *what*?" I pressed.

"He hurt them." As if seeing a memory play out in his mind's eye, Yarik blinked slowly. Between his thighs, he linked his hands together. "He hurt them very bad. They were his best friends, and now they're . . ."

"Dead?" My throat felt too tight.

"No," he said with a sharp shake of his head, "not dead. But he worries, I think, that they want to hurt him as badly as he hurt them."

"So, he thinks they sent me? Is that it?"

"I think he hopes that they did so he has a reason to hurt them even more."

I turned that over in my head, trying to parse out his meaning and read between the lines. It made sense. No matter what I told Petr Volkov, he seemed determined to prove that I had ulterior motives. Maybe they'd all worked together? Clearly, Volkov had betrayed them somehow. But if all that were true, then what could I say to prove my own innocence? I hadn't recognized their photos when Volkov had shown them to me, and I didn't think regaining my memories would change that.

"I ask about you, too," I said, changing the topic. "*Have* asked about you, I mean. No one's said where you were, but I knew that you couldn't be here, not when I've torn this place apart. There aren't any locks on the doors."

"There are locks. Just not on any of the doors you'd come across."

I digested that bit of information, and then said, "What did you do?"

Blond lashes swept down, cutting off access to all that glittering defiance. Against all common sense, I took another step closer to the boy perched atop the suitcase, cataloging every one of his reactions and memorizing them, the way I had already memorized how Volkov flexed just his right hand whenever he was about to lose his cool.

"You did something." Another step closer. "You're the reason I'm still here."

"Has he let you see a doctor again? Your memory should have come back, don't you think?"

"Yarik—"

He blinked up at me, a startled, wide-eyed look that stopped me in my tracks. "Yaroslav."

"What?"

"My name. It's Yaroslav."

"But I thought . . ."

"Yarik is only for—" Lips clamping tight like he'd thought better of it, he bent his knees into his chest, his lanky body suddenly appearing small and unassuming. "It's a nickname. Sort of. Like an endearment."

"In Russian?"

He nodded. "An endearment for Yaroslav, if that makes any sense. For family or close friends. It means something in Russian."

But we weren't in Russia, I knew that much. So, I said, "It means something to *you*."

This time, his cheeks didn't betray a blush, but I could tell the conversation had made him uncomfortable. Somehow, he seemed to curl into himself even tighter. "It does."

"Okay."

"I'm sorry."

"You don't have to be sorry." I tried to smile for him. "You didn't do anything wrong."

"But—"

"Yaroslav, you didn't do anything wrong."

"Maybe one day," he said in that soft, careful voice, "but not yet."

The irony was that he'd cut me off from using a special name that held meaning while I didn't have even a single one to offer him.

Over the last few weeks, I'd tried my best to pick apart my memories; the problem was, I hadn't lied when I said there weren't any from before Yarik—*Yaroslav*—

found me by the river. My reflection said that I wasn't a teenager yet, like Vera, but that I wasn't as young as Yaroslav, either, who Nina had informed me was ten years old. Once I'd showered off the Thames, I'd searched my reflection in the mirror, hoping that there'd be *something* I could latch onto—and there had been in the shape of a thin, vertical scar on my lower abdomen. But whether it was from a past surgery or falling off a bicycle or something else entirely, I didn't remember.

I couldn't remember *anything*.

Though the past haunted me, I didn't feel comfortable bringing any of my concerns to Petr Volkov, not when I thought they might give him more ammunition against me. It was one thing to say that I'd lost my memories—or had them taken from me, more like—and another thing entirely to open up about how confused and frustrated I felt. So, I just bit my tongue, endured our *talks*, and roamed the mansion, looking for the boy who'd saved me.

The boy who kept secrets.

I eyed the suitcase beneath him, still curious. "Can you tell me where you went, at least?"

"Away."

I frowned. "Away? That doesn't explain—"

"Father's going to sit you down tonight. My sister and I won't be there, but I'm not sure about Uncle Igor. Maybe. Depending on Father's mood."

He said it all so fast, as if he had to get the words out before someone strolled in here and tore him away, that I could only keep my mouth shut, determined to give him the floor to say whatever else was clearly on his mind.

Yaroslav hugged his knees. His gaze never left my face. "He's going to say that you have a choice—you don't. He's going to say that if you agree, he'll do whatever he can to help you find your family—he won't. If you stay, you'll be just another soldier to him. Nameless—"

"I don't have a name."

"Everyone has a name," he said with conviction, "you just don't remember yours."

The notion that I might not have always been so alone, without a home or a family, threatened to sweep my feet right out from under me, and I glanced around, heart pounding fast, in search of somewhere to sit. In the end, I went down to the floor. It was only when I lifted my chin and allowed myself to stare into a pair of dark blue eyes that my shallow breathing came even close to evening out.

"Your father . . ." I dug my fingers into the soft rug. "He does bad things, doesn't he?"

"Yes."

"And that's what he wants? From me, I mean. If I become his—"

"Soldier. A Boyevik."

"—I'll do bad things, too?" On the back of that question, another hit me hard, and I heard myself swallow. "Do *you* do bad things?"

He didn't even flinch. "I do what I'm told."

Because even if he was only ten years old, he was still a prince.

Because if Petr Volkov was the one who owned this land, and these trees, and the fucking air we all breathed, then that meant, one day, his son would be the one to inherit it all.

I thought of the weapons I'd found.

I thought of the way Volkov cleaned his gun and his blade and that random kitchen knife, all to intimidate me into spilling secrets that I didn't know because I couldn't remember my own stupid name. He *wanted* to keep me around. Wanted to find, I was sure, a way that I could prove useful to him and whatever bad things he did that could afford him an estate like this one. And if I could help him hurt Cadwell and Kurobara even more, then that was probably just a sweet bonus.

"Why did he come after me? What did you say to him?"

It was Yaroslav's turn to swallow. I heard his throat click and then watched how he adjusted his hold on his knees like it was suddenly too hard to keep still. Finally, he blurted, "He wouldn't have let you live."

My heart squeezed in my chest. "Yaroslav..."

"He would have given you a headstart, just enough to let you think that you'd gotten away, but he would have sent someone to follow. Maybe he'd give you a month or a year, if you were lucky. Enough time for you to find some other place to call home. And then he'd have shot you dead."

Anxiously, I licked my lips. "I don't know anything."

"He wouldn't care."

"I don't even remember my name!" I sounded hysterical, my voice cracking embarrassingly. With trembling fingers, I clutched at my hair, pulling on the strands. "I'm not a threat. I don't have any secrets. I don't even know who I am!"

Those blue eyes turned distraught. "M-maybe I should have let you die."

For the first time, I almost wished he had.

Emotion flooded my veins, and I leaped up, fleeing to the open door like it'd be just as easy to outrun my fate. A fate that no longer belonged to me. Although maybe it never had. Maybe I'd never had a home or a real family, and maybe I was always destined to live a life that belonged to someone else—to never have a name or a past, or anything to call just mine.

It didn't register that I was crying until I heard Yaroslav call after me.

I was already halfway down the hallway when I turned to find him hovering on the threshold of his room, one hand curled into a fist against the doorframe, the expression on his face one that I swore would haunt me until the day I died.

"I'm sorry," he said. "I'm so, so sorry."

I WAS GOING TO RUN.

I'd plotted my escape early on, mapping out various exit points throughout the estate until I had each route memorized. And yet, despite every fiber of my being telling me to get away from this place—from Petr Volkov, specifically—I'd found myself sticking around day after day, for *weeks*, because it felt important that I see Yaroslav one more time before I left for good.

Well, he'd finally come home. And I had just enough common sense rattling around in my skull to realize that if I didn't leave tonight, I might never get another chance to become something other than a killer for a man that I didn't even like.

Turned out that Volkov had given me my own set of guards, just in case I got any wild ideas.

I got no farther than the stables before they caught me and dragged me back to the mansion. They threw me in a cold, dark room, one with a lock on the door. Then they left me alone. I stayed that ways for days—until the fight went out of me, until I lost my voice from screaming, until I folded myself in half, worn down by exhaustion and defeat, and pressed my lips to the strip of space at the base of the door, whispering to whoever was on the other side that I would do anything Petr Volkov asked of me.

When the door finally opened, I learned that I was sorry, too.

CHAPTER FIVE

A week later, I was given the name Kirill.

"After my grandfather," Petr explained, as if I cared. "Kirill Volkov."

I wasn't a Volkov.

I wasn't Kirill.

"Thank you," I said agreeably even though it felt like my entire soul was on fire.

If Volkov realized that I spoke through gritted teeth, he didn't call me out on it. He only pushed his chair back, re-holstered the gun that he'd been methodically cleaning, and motioned for me to get out of his study with a dismissive wave. When I reached the door, he stopped me with a casual, "You'll start learning Russian tomorrow. Fluency is expected from every one of my foot soldiers."

I hesitated for a long, excruciating moment, then forcibly straightened my shoulders and glanced back at the man who'd come to rule my life with an iron fist. My smile was wooden. My heart felt like ice. I'd shatter completely if I let myself. "Of course."

Spine still ramrod straight, I turned to make my escape.

"And Kirill?"

I kept my trembling hands in front of me, out of sight, with my back to the room. They didn't tremble because I was frightened. I was angry. So full of a rage I didn't even understand that it took everything in me to calmly reply, "Yes, sir?"

"Don't think I haven't noticed how my son follows you like a lost puppy."

A vice closed around my lungs, making it hard to breathe.

"Make it stop," Volkov ordered in that quietly terrifying way he had.

"I will, sir."

"Good." There was the sound of shuffling papers. "Thank you for stopping by, Kirill. Close the door on your way out."

"Of course, sir."

I closed the door with a soft *snick* and then smothered a scream by biting down on my bottom lip so hard that I drew blood.

PART TWO
MOSCOW, RUSSIA

CHAPTER SIX
YARIK

"This is *paradise*."

Across the bare dorm room, Kirill dumped his bag on an equally bare bed. His face was stony and unreadable, but that was kind of his thing. "You're delusional."

"I'm not. I just—"

"Have low standards?"

I narrowed my eyes. Then, because I knew he'd let me get away with it—he let me get away with almost everything, honestly—I grabbed a pair of rolled-up socks and chucked them at the back of his head. They didn't make a sound as they dropped harmlessly to the bed. Kirill didn't either, for that matter—just tilted his chin ever so slightly so that he could side-eye me over his shoulder.

I flashed him my most brilliant smile.

His expression didn't even crack, the arsehole.

With a sigh, I flopped backward onto my own bed. So what if the room was barely big enough to fit one person, let alone two, and so what if we were both stuck in Moscow for the foreseeable future? I knew that Kirill didn't lay the blame at my feet even though I secretly thought he should. Instead, he'd been the first to agree that Father's attempt to civilize me—after years spent beating every ounce of civility *out* of me—was bound to end in disaster.

And it had.

The kind of beautiful disaster that included broken bones, an impromptu fire, and my name blacklisted from every boarding school in England.

I bit my bottom lip to keep from grinning.

Not that my paltry attempt at hiding my satisfaction did much good because the next time I blinked, it was on account of Kirill having lobbed the sock-ball back at me. He had great aim. It rebounded off my forehead just as he said, "Don't look so pleased with yourself."

No point in pretending otherwise.

I *was* pretty pleased with myself.

I flipped over onto my stomach, the left side of my face cushioned by a flat, lumpy pillow, and settled in to watch him unpack. "Oh, come on. We both know you're happy to be away from Father."

"I'm only here long enough to get you settled in."

"Maybe I'll take forever, then."

"I can't stay forever. I can't even stay longer than a month."

"A month's a month, isn't it? Better than nothing."

His shoulders flinched at that, and then the ramifications of broken bones, impromptu fires, and my name being blacklisted from now until eternity seemed to hit him all at once, the way it hadn't on the flight over from London, because he abruptly turned around and sat down on the edge of his single bed.

"Fuck," he breathed out, with a slightly flustered glance around the room. "Not much to look at, is it?"

"It's perfect."

He snorted. "Only you'd find perfection in a place like this."

"What's not to love? The wall's crumbling over there." I pointed to his side of the room, which included the doorway that led to what had to be the smallest lavatory in the history of lavatories. "And there's some mold growing, I think, on the window."

Kirill flicked a dubious glance toward the window in question.

"Oh, and there's water damage, too. Look." When he lifted his dark eyes to stare up at the ceiling, and therefore the telltale brown ring of discoloration near the light fixture, I could tell that he was nearing the end of his rope. Which was the only reason I let out a happy sigh—because if I wasn't the one tipping him right over the edge, who would? Half the time he showed all the emotion of a plank of wood. "It's *beautiful*," I gushed, just to mess with him.

For a second, he said nothing.

And then in small, precious increments, the stiff set to his features began to crumble away.

His black brows furrowed, and his dark eyes flashed, and he kicked up his chin the same way he had last year just before he'd tackled me to the ground for daring to put a mouse in his shoe.

"You're taking the piss out of me."

"I'd never."

"*Idi na hui*," he growled without any real heat before grabbing the spare pillow from his bed and throwing that at me, too. I sat up long enough to catch it mid-flight and then made a show of curling back into my spot and tucking it under my head. It was just as lumpy as mine, but whatever. The corner of Kirill's mouth curved. "This place really is shit."

I was suddenly glad for the lumpy pillows. They hid most of my smile. "At least you don't have to deal with Nina for a month."

Dropping his face into the cradle of his hands, Kirill groaned. "Your sister is a menace."

He wasn't being dramatic, either; from the moment he'd entered our lives, my little sister had latched onto him. Two years later and she still wasn't showing any signs of yanking her claws out of his hide anytime soon. It'd become a running joke that if Kirill ever disappeared, Nina would simply evaporate into thin air.

Secretly, I couldn't really blame her.

I'd been following Kirill around for just as long.

I swallowed past the sudden lump in my throat and then did my best to seem casual as I plucked at a loose seam on Kirill's surrendered pillow. "And now you don't have to pretend that you hate me."

The silence that followed was wretchedly oppressive.

Instead of letting his hands drop away from his face, Kirill pushed the heels of his palms against his closed eyelids. I knew that I gave him headaches, sometimes. There wasn't much I wouldn't do to get his attention on me, but I also knew that it wasn't anything I did on purpose that actually irritated him—just my general disposition that made him look like he was fourteen-ish going on forty.

"Tell me that you didn't break Gordon Bethel's arm on purpose," he finally said.

He hadn't moved his hands yet.

That was fine. We could both hide. Wasn't like I'd lifted my face out of my mound of pillows, either.

"I didn't break Gordon Bethel's arm on purpose," I lied.

"Yaroslav."

"And before you ask, I didn't set his room on fire, either."

"*Yaroslav.*"

"What do you want me to say?"

"The truth."

It was my turn to snort. "You never like the truth."

"Give it to me anyway."

"Fine." I swung my legs off of the bed so I could sit up and look him dead in the eye. Or it would have been dead in the eye had he bothered to remove his hands. "You don't like to be stuck on your own as Father's little henchman for long. You hate that whenever I'm sent away to school, all you've got is Nina for company. And Vera, too, I guess, but you hate her as much as I do. Anyway, I made it so that you're not alone." Frowning a little, I gave the room a half-hearted glance of my own. "I mean, I got us sent to what I'm pretty sure is a prison, not a school, but beggars can't be choosers and all that."

That did it.

Kirill's hands fell away from his face, and he stared at me in that earth-shattering way he had. Only seconds under his gaze and I already felt flayed open, skin peeled back from muscle and bone so he could peer into the deepest, most desperate parts of my soul. I always worried about what he might find. I did my best to keep the shadows away from him even when they were wrapped so tight around me, I could hardly breathe.

He gave a disbelieving shake of his head. "You broke a kid's *arm*."

"Technically, he did it himself." Sort of. If by *himself* meant that he'd walked into the cricket bat I'd intended to use on his roommate.

"You lit a fire in his *room*."

Also intended for the roommate, who'd made the unfortunate mistake of trying to bully me whenever we were both in the showers after football practice.

"You got us sent to *Moscow*," Kirill added as if this was my gravest sin, which maybe it was, in his book. In the two years that he'd lived with us, he'd never shown any inclination to visit Russia whenever Father issued an invitation even though he was practically fluent now, and even though not coming meant he stayed behind whenever the rest of us were shepherded onto Father's private jet to make the trip.

Then again, maybe he stayed back because it meant that he was free to look for his family—though he'd never had any luck, from what I knew.

Anyway. Because I was who I was, and Kirill was who *he* was, I only hitched my arms open, as if I was welcoming him into the grandest of palaces. "I got us sent to a *prison* in Moscow," I amended.

His lips twitched as he cut his gaze away.

The silence, this time, was soft and introspective. I could only imagine how he felt to be away from the Volkov compound. Not that we were here alone—I wasn't allowed to go anywhere without my bodyguards, especially not in Russia, where Father's enemies circled like hungry sharks—but he was finally out of Petr Volkov's reach, and there was a chance, even small and temporary as it was, for him to be a teenager for a few weeks instead of the cold-hearted soldier my father was already shaping him into.

When he finally spoke again, his voice was barely above a whisper. "Thank you, Yaroslav."

I remembered the first time he'd thanked me after I'd saved him from the River Thames. He'd pulled me into his arms, then. Hugged me so tight that I actually felt my heels come off the floor. He hadn't touched me since.

"You're welcome," I returned just as softly.

Always, I thought, when he went back to unpacking. And if my heart gave a little squeeze at the thought that it had all been worth it—the broken bones, the fire, the banishment—just to end up here in this tiny room with him halfway around the world, I didn't let myself linger on the feeling for long.

I never did.

CHAPTER SEVEN

KIRILL

It wasn't that I disliked Yaroslav.

I didn't like how impulsive he could be, especially when we both knew he'd inevitably take a beating for it, and I didn't like how quick I always was to stick my own neck out for him and his stupid, hair-brained ideas. After, I always hid the bruises from him well. Wiped my face clean of all emotion, ignored every place on my body that felt scraped raw, and never let Yaroslav Volkov see how deeply he'd buried himself under my skin.

So, no, I didn't dislike him.

But I hated him all the same.

I hated him for dragging me into his world, where I couldn't ever seem to scrub the dried blood clean from under my fingernails, and where I'd learned firsthand what it was like to see the light fade from another man's eyes. I hated that Yaroslav somehow stayed so inherently *good* when I already felt the constant lure of being bad instead.

It was easier to not give a shit about anything than it

was to lie awake in bed each night feeling guilty and ashamed over what I was becoming.

"Now, Kirill."

The order came at me in Russian, as almost everything did these days. I flexed my fingers around the length of rope, made sure the ends were wrapped securely around my knuckles, and applied renewed pressure to the traitor's throat. Immediately, he started thrashing.

"Tighter."

I jerked a questioning glance toward Artem.

"Tighter," he repeated firmly, so I obeyed like the good little foot soldier I was. It didn't matter that the man in the chair had about thirty years on me or that I was barely half his weight. I'd been taught where to lay the rope across the enemy's neck and how to angle my stance so that every escape attempt only made the situation worse.

This situation couldn't get any worse.

Artem strolled closer. Thick-shouldered and brutish, he was Petr's most loyal spy. Or he was now, anyway, since the title previously belonged to the bloke currently zip-tied to the chair.

"Did you think that Volkov wouldn't hear the rumors?" Artem drew to a stop less than an arm's width away. This close, it was impossible to miss how his brown eyes gleamed as he stared down at Pavel Sergerov. "You've gotten sloppy, Sovietnik."

With an angry curse, Volkov's councilor threw himself against the binds, nearly tipping the chair forward onto its two front legs. Thrown off-balance, I dug my heels in and leaned back, using the same brutal technique Sergerov himself had taught me.

It felt wrong.

Wrong, like I was betraying him.

I looked to Artem, stupidly hoping that he might call me off like one of Volkov's dogs that were always kept chained and ready. Artem didn't call me off, though. He didn't even meet my gaze. He was too busy swinging a leg over Sergerov's knees so that he could straddle the older man's lap.

The blade he produced from his waistband shone under the bright lights. As he pressed the tip to Sergerov's chin, I felt my stomach churn uneasily.

"It's theft, what you did." His voice was low, his cadence smooth. The blade danced upward, past the hollow of his cheek to the jut of his browbone. "Stealing product. Working with the Zharkov brothers. Under-mining this family each and every fucking time you draw air into your lying, scheming lungs."

The air left my own lungs as it hit me what Artem planned to do.

It wouldn't be any worse than what I'd already been forced to witness over the last two years. Petr Volkov was a man feared by all despite the fact that he rarely lifted a finger to do the dirty work himself. He didn't have to, not these days. His reputation was the stuff of nightmares, and if I'd learned anything, it was that the only way to survive was to build a wall so tall around my heart that not a single shred of light crept through.

So, while I didn't balk at much these days, I knew Sergerov. He was the closest thing I had to a father. The closest thing I had to a *friend*, besides Yaroslav, and I hadn't realized until this very moment how impossible it was to feel nothing when the only person who'd been remotely kind to me was about to be permanently eradicated.

My hands started to tremble.

And then the worst thing possible happened—Artem noticed.

His gaze sharpened like a predator's, and even though his nostrils didn't exactly flare like a wild animal's tracking the scent of its prey, the shift in his expression had the same effect. My blood went cold and my grip on the rope slackened, giving Sergerov enough leeway to jerk his face away from the knife.

Angrily, Artem slashed his arm in a wide arc.

If it had been anyone else, there would have been a scream, but this was Pavel Sergerov, the same man who'd been shot in the leg last year and dug the bullet out himself, the same man who didn't even bat an eye when his boss, the *pakhan*, suggested that he barter his own nephew's life in a deal to appease the Camorra. Nothing fazed him. *Nothing*. So, it wasn't much of a surprise that having his face sliced in two would only make him grunt.

The surprise came when Artem pushed back onto his feet.

"*Itide syuda.*"

At the command, the tiny hairs on my nape stood on end. I didn't speak. I didn't say anything. My chest rose and fell, quicker and quicker.

"Kirill." There was a new hardness in his tone. It said that I'd be insane to disobey him a second time. "Come here."

There must have been lead in my feet, they felt so heavy. With the rope dangling from one hand, I moved around Sergerov. The tangy scent of blood already permeated the air. It made the swirling unease in my stomach even worse.

"Stand here," Artem directed, except that he placed a hand on my shoulder, where it seemed to burn through the fabric of my pullover, and put me exactly where he wanted me, facing Sergerov head-on. "Now look at him."

I couldn't see anything *but* him—the rope burn around his neck, the straining tension in his shoulders. His shirt gaped in multiple places where the dogs had bitten him when he'd tried to jump a chain-link fence.

Warm fingers suddenly bit into the back of my neck. "I said, *look at him.*"

The first sight of his already craggy face made me feel sick. The blade had cut through the top layers of skin; red shone through. With blood, yes, but the meat of muscle, the white pearl of exposed bone. I swayed on my feet even as Artem held me upright.

Sergerov tried to speak.

Except that he couldn't because his lips were mangled and ruined, and my ears were ringing so loudly that even if he'd managed to get the words out, I wouldn't have heard his mumble anyway.

"This," Artem spat, "is what we do to traitors."

I hated being touched, but I'd fall to the ground if it weren't for the weight of his heavy hand. My heart raced and the air around me practically vibrated with hate— had I hated anyone like this before? Not Yaroslav, who I sometimes resented, but only because I felt the undeniable, confusing rush to keep him safe from even himself. Not even Petr, who I sometimes dreamt of killing before I remembered that without him, I'd probably be in a gutter somewhere, wasting away from starvation and who knows what else.

I didn't understand a hate as fierce as this where I felt it deep in my bones like a poison.

But Artem did.

He seemed to treasure it almost, like a seed planted fresh in the dirt, and I knew deep in my gut that if I didn't nurture that hate, if I didn't water it and do my best to keep it fed, Artem would hate me, too.

"Take this."

I felt myself look down. There was still blood on the blade. It wept from the steel. When I didn't immediately follow through, Artem said again, "Take the knife, Kirill."

I took it.

My fingers felt numb as I turned it over in my hand, wishing that I hadn't already committed its weight to memory.

Artem snatched the rope from my other hand, stalked around me to stand behind Sergerov, and eyed me over the top of Pavel's head. "Put it to his heart."

There was a storm in my ears, wild and utterly ruthless. I felt the aftermath sweep over the length of my body. It left me cold. Mentally absent. I licked my dry lips, trying to find the words to apologize because what else was there to say to a man who was about to die?

I'm sorry that it's you or me.

I'm sorry that you wasted time on me when I'll be the one to kill you.

I'm sorry—I'm sorry—I'm sorry—

I pressed the sharp tip of the blade to Sergerov's heart. Beneath it, his chest hardly moved. Even now, with his face transformed into a beast's, he gave nothing away.

I wondered how far removed from life you had to be to end up this way.

Then again, maybe he was like the stones found in a

riverbed, weathered down by time, growing smaller and smaller until whatever they were before ceased to be. Nothing more than a pebble caught in the rush of the stream.

"Now kill him."

I hadn't killed anyone with my own two hands yet. Somehow, I'd managed to avoid it while operating as Sergerov's shadow.

"Kirill. Now, *kill him.*"

Icy sweat dripped down my nape. I forced myself to look Sergerov in the eye—the one that wasn't closed and swelling. Not sure what I thought I'd find there—maybe a sliver of pity or at least seething rage, but again, there was nothing.

Nothing.

Nothing.

I shoved the blade forward, desperate to see *any* hint of emotion, but—

"Are you fucking worthless?" Artem snapped. "Harder, Kirill. Fucking throw your weight into it."

Killing someone shouldn't have been this difficult. Sergerov, Artem, the others—they all made it look so easy. That wasn't the case here. I was sweating, panting. My palms slid clumsily over the handle of the blade. I thought of Yaroslav doing this at only ten years old. Sergerov gave a shaky whimper, and I didn't know what it said about me that I chased that sound—because with it came the end of this nightmare.

I leaned my weight in.

I stabbed the knife in deep.

A whistling rattle left his lips, like a slowly deflating balloon. He never begged me to change my mind. He didn't even have the fucking decency to look away. I had the feeling that if he'd had the use of his hands, he would have helped me finish the job—because I was taking too long, somehow making a dirty deed less honorable.

Was there any honor in dying in a decrepit warehouse?

Sergerov died without a sound, but inside my soul, there was a terrible, deafening scream.

Before I could even back away, Artem was there, plucking the blade out of my hand and wiping the steel clean on the leg of his jeans. The black material hid the blood well. With a sense of foreboding, I looked down at myself, at the gray pullover I'd thrown on, not knowing what Artem had needed me for when he'd told me to show up here a few hours ago. Blood was splattered across the fabric.

Then I made the mistake of looking down at my feet.

The floor was glossy, a sea of violent red.

I was bent over a second later, wrenching my shoulders away from Sergerov as I unloaded the contents of my stomach with a gasp.

Over the sound of my retching, Artem said, "You'll be heading back to London tomorrow."

Tomorrow?

Still queasy, I lurched upright. "Wait. I thought—"

Artem's hard gaze bored into me. "You thought what?"

A month. I was supposed to be here in Moscow for a month, which meant that I had three weeks left. More than that, actually. I'd only been here for four days. What changed? How did it go from getting Yaroslav settled in at school to—

"Oh."

Artem somehow managed to give the impression of

rolling his eyes without actually doing it. "Yes," he said, "oh. You're just catching on?"

So, this trip had nothing to do with Yaroslav. Instead, it had everything to do with Sergerov, with *killing* Sergerov, and for some reason, Volkov thought it money well spent to send me all the way to Russia to make sure the job got done.

I felt sick.

Artem clapped a bloody hand on my shoulder. "This is what happens to traitors, Kirill. Remember that."

Two years.

I'd spent two years under the thumb of the Russian Bratva, learning their language and adapting their customs, only to be forced to commit murder, all so I'd be reminded that while I might have been the councilor's shadow, I was no better than every other foot soldier they took under their wing—a faceless killer who only held value for as long as he remained loyal to the *pakhan*. Betraying that oath guaranteed you a fate like Sergerov's.

Dead in a decrepit warehouse.

No friends, no family.

"Do you understand?" Artem squeezed my shoulder.

You aren't special, went unspoken.

You are replaceable like all the others.

I didn't need to look at Sergerov to know my answer. "Yes, I understand."

CHAPTER EIGHT

YARIK

It was almost two in the morning when the door finally cracked open and a sliver of light from the hallway spilled into the room.

I'd turned off the overhead light almost an hour ago. It was easier to not look so desperate in the dark.

I held my breath as Kirill stumbled his way into the toilet. The door closed behind him, and seconds later, the shower went on. He'd been gone for hours. I wasn't sure where, and he hadn't given much information besides meeting up with one of Father's brigadiers. It was ridiculous to think that he'd come all this way to Moscow and wouldn't be expected to work.

Ridiculous, but somehow, I'd tricked myself into thinking just that.

Father had an entire enterprise here in Russia, the same as in London. His currency of choice was guns. Big ones, small ones, automatic ones. He told me that I was still too young to know anything about his clients, which always struck me as a weird thing to say because he clearly didn't think I was too young to know what it felt like to kill someone.

That was Petr Volkov logic for you, though. Totally warped.

Still, I was smart enough to put the pieces together. I knew that on certain days of the week, there were foreign politicians who stopped by, dressed in their crisp suits with their shiny watches that peeked out from beneath starched cuffs. They brought bodyguards, too, which never really seemed to put them at ease. On other days, there were still men in crisp suits and shiny watches, but they always came alone and they rarely, if ever, looked anything short of arrogant. These men breezed in, offered back-thumping hugs for my father, and left an hour or two later with a pep in their step.

I figured that my father had a way of either making your dreams come true . . .

Or making you wish that you'd never been born.

So, I should have known that he wouldn't let Kirill come all this way just for me. Father kept him on a short leash—no school, just real-life lessons that pertained to business, paired with rigorous physical training that had already started to thicken Kirill's shoulders. I was still taller, but in every other way, I wasn't sure how much longer I'd remain bigger. Something about that made me feel good. I didn't like the thought of Kirill always looking underfed, like wherever he'd come from had made food hard to come by.

The sound of running water cut off, followed by the near-silent thump of feet hitting the old, uneven flooring.

When he opened the door a few minutes later, I slid a closed fist under my pillow. I watched silently as he shuffled around in the darkness, tugging on clothes, throwing back the thin bedsheet. He hovered there a second as if he was debating getting into bed, before I heard him swallow and sit down heavily. The old mattress squeaked as he lay down.

There was barely any space between us.

If I reached out a hand, I could almost touch his nightstand.

Something was wrong. From the moment I'd found him, I'd developed a weird sort of sixth sense to everything that made him *him*. Most of the time, it meant that I could predict his moods as easily as I could predict the possibility of a gray, London day. Had something happened when he'd gone to meet Artem? Or was it something else, like that one time I'd found him pacing in the middle of the night, anxious over a dream he'd had that made no sense?

He flipped over onto his back.

I clutched my pillow even tighter like it was the only thing grounding me to the bed.

Moments later, he turned onto his side to face the wall. If I tried hard enough, I could almost see the shape of his shoulders—

Was he crying?

"Kirill." In the quiet of our room, my voice was a breathless, vibrating mess. When he didn't answer, I nearly threw myself at him. "*Kirill.*"

"Not right now." It was barely above a whisper. *Barely.* "Please."

Yeah, not happening.

I launched out of the bed and nearly got taken out by a rogue pair of trainers I'd forgotten to put away. Kicking them aside, I crossed the four measly steps that separated our living quarters, but all my bravado fled the moment I was close enough to touch him. Because that was the one thing my sixth sense never failed to pick up—

Kirill did not like to be touched.

It went against every human instinct, but I slid down to the floor, pressing my spine against the side of his bed and wrapping my arms tight around my knees.

The mattress squeaked again. "What are you doing?"

"Waiting."

"For what?"

"For you to tell me who hurt you."

The sheets rustled like he was tucking himself into a tight ball. He was still facing the wall. I only knew it because when he spoke, his voice was muffled as if he was speaking in the opposite direction. "No one hurt me. Go to bed."

"*Someone* did," I said, a little more angrily than I'd intended. "You don't cry—ever."

He hesitated, a long, heavy pause that bled from one second into the next. And then, stiffly, like he was desperate to make it true: "I'm not crying."

"Sure."

"I'm *not*."

"We're mates, aren't we? I'm not going to make fun of you if you are. Promise."

I didn't know what I expected when it wasn't as if Kirill ever gushed over me. I annoyed him, I knew, and I frustrated him to the point where sometimes I felt how badly he wanted to shut me up, but that didn't mean we . . . that we weren't . . . "We *are* friends, aren't we?"

The silence that followed made me want to crawl out of my skin. It wasn't just heavy, like the other day, but something perilously close to pure torture. If there'd been a Grandfather's clock in here, like there was back home, I could have counted every passing second. As it was, there wasn't anything for me to do but try not to squirm as I fell into the awful decision of counting out our breathing instead. We weren't in sync. Every time I inhaled, he exhaled, and every time he drew in a breath, I seemed to choke on mine as I let it out in a rush.

I swallowed. "Kirill?"

"You don't let me call you Yarik."

"What?"

"You said, family and friends call you Yarik. It means something to you, you said. So, no, we aren't mates."

My jaw dropped open. "I didn't—what I mean is—"

"It's fine." More shuffling came from behind me. "*I'm* fine. Go to bed."

"*No.*" I whipped around. Before I could stop myself, I'd sat myself on his bed, as far away from him as I could possibly get without falling off the mattress. "No, it's not fine. You think that I don't know how many times you've gotten into trouble for me? You think I haven't noticed how you watch me whenever Father is around, like you're one step away from throwing yourself between us, just to keep him away from me?"

"Yaroslav—"

"*No*, Kirill. No. I'm tired of feeling like I have to beg you to pay me the slightest bit of attention when we both know that you already are!" I was breathing too fast, worked up with no outlet but the boy who now sat back against the headboard, the sheets pooled around his waist while he watched me unload two years of feelings into the empty space between us. "And you don't think— you don't think that *I* notice everything about you, too? Who do you think got Pavel to take you on when it was obvious to *everyone* that the moment Father looks your way, you shrivel up? And who do you think convinced Pavel to let you—"

"He's dead."

I jerked my chin back. "What?"

"He's *dead*. Pavel. He's dead and I—" There was a terrible noise. A high-pitched whine, not unlike a dying animal. Kirill clapped his hands over his mouth as if he could keep the sound locked inside his soul, tamped down and forgotten.

Slowly, I shifted onto my knees.

If it was possible, he angled himself even farther away until he was shoved into the corner of the bed where the frame met the wall. But he never took his hands away from his mouth, and the wide-eyed look in his gaze told me that he was terrified to make that sound again.

Pavel was dead.

The news pinged around my brain. I didn't know how I felt about that. Pavel Sergerov was—had been—a gruff, middle-aged man whose bark was just as bad as his bite, but I'd always liked him anyway. He'd never hit me. He'd never yelled at me—much—and whenever I pestered him with questions, he'd always dropped to his haunches, looked me dead in the eye like I was worth something, and gave me his all.

I'd begged him to take Kirill away from Father.

Begged and begged and begged until he'd grabbed me by the scruff of my shirt, hoisted me in the air, and dumped me in a spare room with a lock on the door. The last thing I'd heard before he'd walked away was, "Volkovs do not beg, *patsan*."

But he'd done it, hadn't he? Whatever he said to Father worked because the very next day, Kirill was permanently assigned to be Pavel's shadow, and that was a big thing, seeing as Pavel was my father's right-hand man.

I worried my bottom lip. "What happened?"

Kirill shook his head almost frantically.

Nerves wound their way down my spine, unraveling like a ball of electricity until even the tips of my toes felt tingly. Somewhere, in the back of my head, I knew where this was going, but I needed him to say it. To own it. He'd never get past this if he couldn't.

Carefully, I said, "Did he do something bad?"

That animalistic whine again, followed immediately by Kirill slamming his eyes shut.

I licked my dry lips. "Did *you* do something bad?"

He sank down into his place against the wall, his shoulders creeping up toward his ears, like he could disappear if only he tried hard enough. He gave a painfully slow nod that I almost missed.

"Okay," I whispered gently. "Okay. Did you . . . Did you have a choice?"

Instead of answering, his fingers seemed to grip his mouth even harder. If the lights had been on, I knew there'd be prints left on his skin when he finally pulled away. As it was, there was just enough illumination from the curtain-covered window for me to see how his black eyes glistened with unshed tears.

I licked my lips again. "Will you let me come closer? I won't touch you. I won't, I promise."

The moment he nodded, I scooted as close as I dared. There was still a good two feet between us. But it felt close enough—*safe* enough—for me to keep my voice soft and soothing as if I was telling him a secret.

"I didn't have a choice, either. It wasn't . . ." I closed my eyes for just a second, trying to breathe steadily past my thundering heart. "It was a gun that felt too big in my hand, and Father standing right there behind me—I could feel his breath, you know? On the back of my neck. He didn't think I'd do it, but we both knew that if I didn't, bad things would happen. I was crying. It made him angry. Nothing new there, I guess. I always make him angry."

I shifted so I could sit cross-legged with my hands resting on my ankles. "I didn't know the bloke's name. I wondered about that, whether it was easier not knowing. But then I got thinking, what if he's got someone he loves? What if he's got a whole family? And I said it, without thinking, *Do you love someone*, because it seemed like something I ought to know, but what was I really gonna do? Go to his house and say a nine-year-old killed your dad? Stupid."

Stupid, stupid, stupid.

"It didn't matter, anyway, in the end. Father got so bloody angry, I could—I could *feel* it, and then he wrapped his hand around mine and made me pull the trigger. Bloke died before he could tell me."

Kirill was watching me closely. It wasn't one of his earth-shattering stares but something else entirely. Like he didn't know whether to close the gap between us or go running for the door. I wondered if he ever laid in bed at night wishing for a hug.

I did.

No one ever hugged me, and I felt starved for it.

"So, I know how you feel right now, and it's okay if you—"

"It's worse." The ragged confession emerged like it'd been torn from his soul. "It's worse to . . . to know like I knew."

That made sense. The knowing was always worse than the wondering. "It gets easier."

"You're lying to me," he said, still burrowed in his corner. "Don't lie to me."

"Fine. Okay." I ran my sweaty hands across my thighs. "It gets worse, but you also get better at putting the Bad Things into a box. That's what I do. I put it all in a box in my head, and I turn the key, and then, I walk away."

Or I try to find you.

I didn't say that, though. I didn't have the balls. But just because I knew how to keep my mouth shut didn't mean that I didn't think it, that I didn't *feel* it. And I felt a whole lot when it came to Kirill Volkov.

Something about him drew me like a moth to a flame, which was only a problem because most of the time, he looked at me as if he couldn't ever trust me, as if he didn't even *like* me, when all I saw in *him* was safety. A place to lay down my head and rest, knowing that he'd have my back while I slept.

I wanted to know what that felt like—to sleep without worry. It sounded like an impossible dream.

Feeling strangely empty, I got off the bed and wrapped my arms around myself. "Put it in a box, okay? And I'm here, you know. For the next month, at least." I tried for a crooked grin but doubted it got anywhere past a grimace.

I'd just gotten a knee on my mattress when I heard his squeal in protest. I looked back at him, because of course I did, only to find shadows sliding over his frame as he reached out a hand toward me.

If it had been daylight, he never would've done that. Too vulnerable. Too exposing. A thin strip of moonlight illuminated the curve of his hand, the trembling stretch of his fingertips. So, it was a good thing that it was the middle of the night when secrets spilled out into the open and nightmares rose up from the grave. It made the fact that I wanted to take his hand in mine okay. We could forget all about it tomorrow, couldn't we? My heart pounded so hard, it threatened to steal the breath right out of my lungs.

"Don't go," he whispered. "Please . . . don't go."

The plea was desperate, soft. I didn't have the willpower to stay away when all I'd ever wanted was for him to need me the same way I almost always seemed to need him.

I didn't utter a word in return.

Just grabbed the blanket from my bed and took my place at the foot of his, content to guard him while he slept. It felt right, sitting here. It felt like fate.

CHAPTER NINE

KIRILL

I didn't tell Yaroslav about me leaving Moscow.

He knew the score. Same way he knew my place in the Volkov organization—at the bottom of the ladder with all the other foot soldiers but a rung above the traitors. Traitors like Pavel Sergerov.

I tried to do as he said, though. I went back to London with a brand-new box in my head, one with a latch that I kept locked at all times. It made things strangely easy when Volkov sat me down to ask me about my trip.

"Artem passed your message along," I said as if I hadn't broken down in front of his son less than twenty-four hours earlier.

"Good," Volkov replied.

And that was that.

Good meant that I was given more responsibilities.

Good meant that I was trusted.

Good did not mean that I was suddenly a member of the family. That was a lesson I'd already learned the hard way. I was not Kirill, and I would never be a Volkov. Maybe Petr would take pity on me since he'd forced me to kill the one person who had cared about my welfare, but there was no doubt in my mind that any mercy he extended my way would only go so far.

After all, I might live in their home, but I was still just a soldier.

Like a stray brought in from the cold, but only when it suited them. One that they paraded about like a prized bull, lauded when the situation called for it, and then abandoned on the front stoop as soon as their guests departed for the night. Always on the outside looking in with my hand pressed to the icy window, wondering if I'd ever be lucky enough to be invited inside to thaw out in front of the fire.

I wasn't holding my breath.

Two weeks after I got back, Artem pressed a mobile into the palm of my hand, the look on his face suggesting that he'd smelled something rotten.

"What's this for?" I asked.

"A fucking gift," he snapped back before stalking off down the hall.

I turned it over in my hand, then scrubbed my thumb across the cracked screen. It wasn't anything like the newer models I'd seen Volkov with, and there was a suspicious dent in one corner that said it'd made contact with a hard surface or two, but it was . . . Well, it was mine now, wasn't it? Nothing had ever been just mine before, and I found myself clutching it to my chest like it was priceless.

When it vibrated a few hours later, I pulled it from my pocket to find a new notification winking at me. An unknown number. The text consisted of just two words, but they turned my world upside down:

It's Yarik.

PART THREE
SPLIT IN TWO

CHAPTER TEN

YARIK

Do you have a favorite constellation?

KIRILL

. . . no.

YARIK

Really?

KIRILL

I really don't.

YARIK

So, you're going to tell me that you never go out at night just to look up at the stars?

I'm outside right now, in case you're wondering.

KIRILL

I wasn't.

YARIK

But if you were . . .

Play the game?

KIRILL

Fine.

What are you doing outside? It's two in the morning there.

Deleted Kirill Text:

In fucking February. Go inside before you get sick or someone puts a gun to your

YARIK

Sometimes I come outside to look up at the stars, so it won't feel like I'm so far away from home. Sometimes I like to think that I could reach up and steal one from the sky. Hold it in the palm of my hand and pretend someone back home will realize it's gone missing.

I lay down, too, even when it's cold like it is tonight. I want to feel alive but I

KIRILL

But what?

Yarik. But you WHAT?

Deleted Yarik Text:
I feel so alone

YARIK

But then I remember that I don't really know anything about stars or galaxies or constellations, so I borrowed a book from the library.

Deleted Kirill Text:
Tell me what you wanted to say

YARIK

I'll tell you all about it if I ever get around
to reading it.

KIRILL

You do that.

I've got to get back to work.

YARIK

Okay.

Night, Kirill.

KIRILL

Good night, Yarik.

Deleted Yarik Text:
How do you make friends?

I hate it here.

YARIK

All right. I found it.

KIRILL

Found what?

YARIK

My favorite constellation.

Well, I mean, I haven't found it in the sky
but it's my favorite story so far. Ready?

KIRILL

Do I have a choice?

YARIK

Do you ever?

KIRILL

Fine. Lay it on me.

YARIK

Are you sitting down? You should be
sitting down for this.

KIRILL

I'm literally scrubbing someone's blood
out of your father's precious eighteenth-
century floor.

YARIK

So, you're on your knees? That
works, too.

KIRILL

Piss off.

YARIK

Good to know you're as grumpy as ever.

KIRILL

You going to tell me your story, or what?
Someone's gonna start asking questions
when I'm not done in here soon.

YARIK

Oh, right.

So, there was once a queen

KIRILL

Is this a fairy tale? Are you making it all up?

YARIK

Arsehole. I was gathering my thoughts!

KIRILL

Well, hurry up on the gathering. I can hear Artem down the hall.

YARIK

Who died, anyway?

KIRILL

Does it matter?

YARIK

Guess not.

So, there was once this ancient Egyptian queen. When her husband, Ptolemy, went off to war, she was so worried that he might not come back that she actually cut off her blonde hair.

KIRILL

Wow.

All of it? Just a strand? Tell me everything.

YARIK

You're taking the piss out of me.

Deleted Kirill Text:
You're too easy to mess with

KIRILL
Yarik,

YARIK
Yeah?

KIRILL
Keep going.

YARIK
It's said that her hair was the pride of Egypt. She laid it across the Temple of Aphrodite as a sacrifice. Anything to bring Ptolemy home.

It worked, I guess.

Aphrodite was so struck by the queen's love for her husband that she made sure Ptolemy survived the battle and made his way home safely. Then she took the queen's sacrifice and used it to decorate the sky, giving us stars that shine bright like spun gold.

Are you still there?

You haven't said anything.

KIRILL
Trying to understand why that one's your favorite.

Deleted Yarik Text:
I don't know. Or maybe I do. It's just that, when I came across it, I couldn't help but stare at myself in the mirror.

I'd shave my hair, too, if I was like the queen, praying for the person I loved to come back to me. I'd sacrifice a lot more than my hair, I think. I'd do just about anything to keep them safe. Thinking like that keeps me up at night. I haven't slept. It's this place. It's so cold, Kirill. Cold and lonely and

YARIK

I like that the king found his way home.

KIRILL

Yaroslav, you know . . .

You know that you can come back to London, don't you? Volkov would let you.

Yarik?

Bloody hell, Yarik. Just answer me.

KIRILL

Stop being a brat.

You think I don't know how much you miss England?

You think I don't know that the reason you're texting me at all hours of the night is because you're fucking choking on regret after being so impulsive?

Deleted Kirill Text:
I hate that about you

You got yourself shipped off to the other side of the world
and now I'm losing sleep because of you

KIRILL

Put your pride down and tell your father
that you want to come home.

YARIK

I already did.

KIRILL

And?

YARIK

He said no.

KIRILL

Look up the constellation Andromeda.

YARIK

Okay.

Soooo, this one's dark.

KIRILL

Not really.

YARIK

She's almost devoured by a sea monster.
How is that not dark?

KIRILL

But she's saved, isn't she? Perseus saves
her on his white steed.

YARIK

The white steed has a name.

KIRILL

Pegasus, I know.

Did you get to the part where she and
Perseus get married?

YARIK

Yup.

KIRILL

And?

YARIK

She spent her childhood chained up by
her parents. Then she almost gets eaten
by the sea monster. And then she just,
what, gets saved and ends up married to
the bloke who rescued her???

KIRILL

That bloke ends up being king.

YARIK

So, she's essentially chained to a throne
as his queen. Sounds fun.

KIRILL

Says the mafia prince.

YARIK

Maybe that's how I know she's traded
one set of chains for another.

KIRILL

If Volkov ever hears you say that…

YARIK

Why do you think I'm still in Moscow?

Deleted Yarik Text:
You're going to think I'm so stupid

I'm at this party, and I wish you were here. I don't even know why I haven't left except

Okay, I know why I haven't left. I told myself that I'd come for an hour and try to be normal. These kids don't know that the best way to stab someone is under the rib cage in a sharp, upward motion. But they know what it's like to kiss someone and I have no idea what that's like. I wish I did. I wish I was interested in any of the girls that are here.

I just keep thinking about how much I miss

YARIK

Have you kissed someone before?

KIRILL

What?

YARIK

Kissing. Have you had your first kiss yet?

KIRILL

How's that any of your business?

YARIK

You're my best mate.

KIRILL

And?

YARIK

Shouldn't I know everything about you?

KIRILL

No.

YARIK

Well, you know everything about me.

Deleted Kirill Text:

That's because you never stop talking. You don't even give me a chance to breathe before your brain's flitting off to another topic. I could list off a thousand things that I know about you and there'd still be another thousand that I could mention

KIRILL

Why do you want to know if I've kissed someone?

YARIK

I want to know what it's like.

KIRILL

So go and find out.

YARIK

You're really not going to tell me?

KIRILL

I don't actually have to tell you everything.

YARIK

Huh.

KIRILL

. . . huh, what?

YARIK

I don't think you've done it.

KIRILL

Done what?

YARIK

Kissed somebody.

I really thought you would have by now. Not because being sixteen is old, or whatever, but because you're too curious. You don't like being kept in the dark. The not knowing scares you.

KIRILL

Yarik . . .

YARIK

But maybe you haven't because you don't actually trust anyone. Kissing means closing your eyes. It means letting down your guard and holding someone close enough that you can feel their heartbeat against your chest.

You can't kiss someone with a knife in your hand.

KIRILL

Says who?

YARIK

Someone, probably. I bet it's a rule.

KIRILL

I could kiss someone with a knife in my hand. If I wanted to.

YARIK

Sources say no.

KIRILL

Bloody hell. Are you ASKING someone???

Deleted Yarik Text:
Who would I even ask?

YARIK

Should I?

KIRILL

NO.

YARIK

I can. I'm at a party and there are a ton of people here. Someone would be able to tell me what's the right sort of etiquette for kissing.

I bet they'd tell me all the ways that you're wrong.

I'm definitely going to ask. You've gotten a big head, Kirill. Someone needs to bring you back down to earth.

KIRILL

Fuck, you're a menace.

Yes, I've kissed someone.

Deleted Yarik Text:
Oh

When did this happen?

Are you dating her?

Is she there with you right now?

> YARIK
>
> Did you like it?

> > KIRILL
> >
> > It wasn't bad, I guess.

> YARIK
>
> But it wasn't good??

> > KIRILL
> >
> > It was fine.

> YARIK
>
> Sources say that doesn't sound like a ringing endorsement.

> > KIRILL
> >
> > Sources say that mafia princes ought to mind their own fucking business.

> YARIK
>
> I'm going to go find someone to kiss. It's going to be better than fine. I just know it.

Deleted Yarik Text:
I couldn't do it.

I couldn't because I can't stop thinking about

I wish you hadn't had your first kiss already

CHAPTER ELEVEN

YARIK

I became something of a masochist over the next year.

It wasn't like I set out to find ways to make myself feel as if I was dying inside, but as it turned out, I was pretty good at holding the knife and drawing blood.

Take the second, third, and fourth times that I tried to kiss someone. There were a few girls in my year who liked my posh English accent—their words, not mine—I sounded nothing like the rich toffs who did business with my father—and the fact that I stood taller than all the other boys probably scored me a few points, too. The thing was, I was a bit of an anomaly. No one actually wanted to get to know me, but girls still passed me notes in class, writing things like:

Go to a party with me on Friday?

I like your eyes. Is that a weird thing to say?
It's just that they're such a pretty blue.

Sit next to me tomorrow?

Sometimes, I dragged myself out to whatever party was happening because it beat staying home alone in my moldy room; I didn't understand the obsession with blue eyes when I couldn't ever seem to stop thinking about a pair of black ones that glittered with distrust—and I never, ever took up the offer to move seats.

I kept to myself for the most part.

At first, it was because I didn't see the point in making friends when I'd eventually be sent back to England, but then one month turned into two, and three turned into four, and soon, it became glaringly obvious that Father had no intention in calling me back home. By that point, I'd garnered the reputation of being a loner.

No one wanted to be friends with a loner.

Or maybe it was that no one wanted to be friends with a loner like me.

Thanks to my father, everyone knew the Volkov name, and everyone feared it. I was a pariah, in part because I didn't know how to bridge the gap between me and my classmates, and also because I couldn't actually erase the blood that ran through my veins, despite how good I was at suffocating myself in the hurt.

"Excuse me," one of the boys in my year said as he shoved past me. He didn't lift his gaze to meet mine—not that I thought he would. The girls still flirted with me, but the boys kept their distance. They always had.

It bothered me.

Made me want to act out, to bare my teeth, or do something drastic like push them up against a wall. Except that my back was already up against a wall, literally, and by the time I got my mouth open to tell him to piss off, Isaak had already disappeared into the crowd.

Frustration welled up inside me.

Before I could stop myself, I was following him.

Just because I was a loner didn't mean that I was invisible. I couldn't even breathe at school without attracting unwanted attention. Even here, on nights like this, when adults were scarce and mayhem lingered on the horizon, I still couldn't hide in the shadows. Maybe it was because of my size or maybe it was on account of my face—I was rubbish at managing my expressions—but everyone slunk aside to let me pass through. Their wariness only made me grit my teeth even harder.

I shouldn't have bothered coming out tonight, simple as that. Courtesy of today's go-round with my sperm donor, there was a perpetual black cloud hanging over my head. I felt trapped. Scraped raw emotionally while still flying high on the wings of fury, the way I always did after a call with daddy dearest.

I hadn't been home in almost three years. He'd told me that I wouldn't be welcome back for another three if I didn't get my head out of my arse. Which was all kinds of ironic, if you asked me, because there wasn't anything my father hated more than spineless twats, and yet he expected me to roll over like an obedient dog.

You'll live here until I tell you otherwise—

You'll do what I say when I say it—

You'll marry—

I caught a glimpse of Isaak's brown hair.

Maybe it was the thrill of the chase or maybe it was the chance to finally tell him to take his attitude and shove it up his arse, but either way, my palms were sweating as I followed him into the garden behind the house. It was one of the nicest properties I'd ever seen. Dark-stained wood finishes that matched the surrounding tree line. Besides the jacuzzi that sat under an ornate pergola, it was impossible to miss the three massive fireplaces with their black marble mantles that ran up alongside the house. Teenagers had overtaken the seating area, jostling each other as they laughed. Isaak briefly joined them before slipping off into the night, his silhouette immediately lost amongst the trees.

I stood there a second, my breath lodged like a second pulse in my throat.

Then I fumbled for my phone, hating myself even as I thumbed past my thread with Kirill to the one directly below it. It felt like I'd been yanked right out of my body as I stared down at the picture Vera had sent me an hour ago.

I wanted to throw the device across the garden.

Smash it against one of those black marble mantles.

Watch it burn in the fire and feel nothing when it went up in flames.

VERA

I guess he cleans up okay.

She didn't need to include any other context because I knew it all from today's call with Father. I knew that he was hosting a party at our country estate. I knew that he'd invited everyone short of the royal family—and he would've invited them, too, but he'd recently gotten into it with one of the princes. And I knew that he'd told Kirill to bring a date.

Objectively, she was beautiful.

Objectively, her black hair was long and shiny, pinned up with blue ribbons that matched her dress, and the way she stared up at Kirill with stars in her eyes belonged on a film poster at the cinema.

Objectively, I hated her.

I didn't look at Kirill before shoving my phone back into the pocket of my jeans. I didn't memorize every change the last two and a half years had left on his familiar face. And I definitely didn't touch the tip of my finger to the corner of his unsmiling mouth and wonder if he already knew how she tasted.

Objectively speaking, I was a fucking liar.

Beneath my feet, the world felt lopsided. The trees grew crooked, and the moon rose from the earth. I couldn't seem to catch my breath. I couldn't make the hurt *stop*. I stumbled away from the house toward the jagged tree line. The cold air stung my exposed skin, so I hugged my arms to my chest while the soles of my trainers crunched on dead leaves.

I wasn't looking for Isaak, but I wasn't not looking for him either.

I was almost fifteen years old, and I'd never been kissed. The girls who flirted with me made a pit open in my stomach. I let them touch me—a hand on my chest, a shoulder pressed against mine—because it seemed like something I should do, and I'd been raised to obey or face the consequences. The boys, like Isaak, wanted nothing to do with me, for reasons I didn't understand. I dressed like them. I spoke Russian like them. I loved playing football, same as they did, and I could out-bench all of them if I wanted. But none of them offered friendship, and they continued to avoid me like I had poison running through my veins.

The quiet hum of voices up ahead slowed my footsteps.

I'd spent enough time hunting both two and four-legged prey to know how to quiet my approach so I didn't make a sound. I slipped through the shadows as I'd done a million times before, moving from the trunk of one tree to the next until I had a clear view.

A girl had joined Isaak.

Her hair was blond like mine, but long, reaching all the way down to the small of her back. Isaak had the strands wrapped around his fist, but there wasn't any violence in the gesture. He was . . . flirting. His green eyes shone like brilliant emeralds under a patch of moonlight, and his teeth were a flash of white as he threw back his head with a low, happy laugh.

The girl rose onto her toes as she pressed her hands to the center of his chest. She laughed, too, this tinkling, delicate sound that didn't grate on my nerves so much as it made my heart race even faster. Not because I was entranced. Not even because I wanted her. But because I couldn't help but wonder what it would be like to take her place.

To feel the tree bark scrape my skin.

To have a boy I liked play with my hair.

To know in my heart that someone wanted me as much as I wanted them.

I didn't know what that was like, and I craved it. Was *desperate* for it.

A ragged sigh left my lips. I wouldn't have thought anything of it, but winter crept closer every day, and the woods weren't alive with the sounds of summertime. There was me, and there was Isaak and the girl, and I didn't even have the chance to hide before Isaak's gaze found me within the shadows and went hard.

Run, run, run.

I was frozen in place, terrified to make a sound.

Realizing that something was wrong, the girl turned her head to follow the direction of Isaak's stare. The moment she spotted me, her eyes went round, bulging in surprise, and Isaak let go of her hair to angle her face into his chest, as if I was . . . as if I was something *wrong*.

A creep.

Some monster hiding in the woods.

I opened my mouth and stumbled backward at the same time, wanting to defend myself while also desperate to run far, far away. Escape won out, in the end. Self-preservation always did.

With a broken gasp, I spun around and sprinted as fast as my legs could carry me. The cold settled like icy fingers around my lungs, squeezing, squeezing, squeezing, until the edges of my vision blurred and misery howled in my ears.

When I reached the bus stop, I drew too much attention getting on, so I quickly found an empty seat and turned toward the smudged window, trying my best to ignore the mottled reflection staring back. I didn't recognize myself. Not the windswept blond hair or the flushed cheeks, and definitely not the haunted gaze.

There were tear tracks on my cheeks.

I didn't recognize those either.

My room was empty, the same way it'd been since the day Kirill went back to London.

I stripped off my jeans and crawled into bed without brushing my teeth. I didn't have the energy tonight. If I was being really honest with myself, it was worse than that; I didn't want to run the risk of looking at myself in the mirror, of meeting the gaze of the broken boy who dwelled in the lost crevices of my soul, who begged for scraps after years spent locked away in the darkness.

I'd tried destroying him.

Drew blood and let him weep onto the floor, hoping with every cut that he would disappear for good. But he lived within me always, a needy, hopeful thing that threatened every corner of my life with his inability to just stay *gone*.

Chills wracked my frame as I drew the thin blanket over my head. Facts were facts. I was stuck in Moscow. Maybe forever but at least for now. *Unless you stop fighting and do what he wants.*

I wouldn't.

I fucking *refused*.

Curling into a tight ball, I kept my back to the empty room and prayed for sleep. It came in wretched spurts, my dreams plagued by nightmares that kept me from falling deeper, until finally, I gave up, throwing the covers aside and tugging my jeans back on. It was cold when I stepped outside but no colder than my heart as I made my way to the spot I loved beneath the stars.

I lay down in the dead grass.

Tipped my head back on the pillow of my bent arm.

It was only then, when I was shivering but bathed in pale moonlight, that I reached for my phone. Out here, I could pretend that I wasn't so very alone. Out here, I could stare up at the night sky and convince myself, if only for a little while, that I wasn't drowning. I pulled up Kirill's last text and read it out loud to the stars:

"Happy birthday, Yarik."

CHAPTER TWELVE
KIRILL

I was on cleanup duty when he rang.

We didn't do that, Yarik and me. Over the last few years, we'd fallen into the habit of texting around the clock, but I couldn't tell you the last time I'd heard the sound of his voice. It was my fault. I'd grown used to dealing with men like Petr Volkov, who expected that I—along with all the other lowly soldiers in his well-oiled cog—be seen, not heard. Against all better judgment, I'd turned into a glorified mercenary. Good for killing but otherwise told to blend in with the wallpaper.

Some days I never spoke at all.

I forced myself to put my mobile away. I'd phone him back, I would. First, I had to get rid of a body.

My hands slid over bloodied flesh as I dragged Jocle Stevens onto a large, black tarp. Fuck, he was heavy. Didn't help that, thanks to being shot point-blank by yours truly, he was the literal definition of dead weight. I arranged his arms down by his sides, tucked the tarp under his still-warm body, and rolled him over until he was cocooned by the material. Sitting back on my haunches, I wiped the inside of my wrist across my sweaty forehead.

I hated this part.

With a grunt, I hoisted good ol' Jocle over my shoulder, only to stagger sideways under his bulk, barely catching myself before I went down with him on top of me. Tightening my core, I dug my fingers into what might have been his thighs and then shuffled my way toward the warehouse's exit. Just because I didn't have Artem watching my every move tonight didn't mean that I couldn't hear him reaming me out in my head.

The fuck are you doing taking so long?

Move faster, Volkov, before I get rid of you.

Stop being a lazy cunt.

I wasn't a lazy cunt. I was the youngest soldier in Volkov's entire organization and still took on more responsibilities than men twice my age. Artem had long since beaten any trace of hesitation out of me. He seemed to take pride in it—the way I no longer thought twice about pulling a trigger or palming a blade. But still, he found ways to provoke me, always speaking down to me as if I was the dirt caked on the bottom of his shoe.

It did something to me, that barely concealed revulsion. Lit a fuse in my soul that never went away, not even when I was doing grunt work like this, disposing of the body of some nobody drug lord whose only mistake was thinking that he could do business on territory Volkov coveted but didn't own. Didn't own *yet*, at any rate. There wasn't much of London that Petr didn't have his eye on.

I had the body half-loaded into the car when my back pocket vibrated. The vehicle groaned with Jocle's added weight as I dumped him the rest of the way in, then slammed the boot shut. Snagging my phone, I checked the cracked screen and immediately felt myself stiffen as I answered.

"I'm on my way."

Artem didn't miss a beat. "You're late."

I wasn't. This was just another one of his pointless mind games where he poked and prodded, hoping I'd do something stupid enough to get my arse handed to me by the boss. There weren't such things as angels in the Bratva, but sometimes, I thought that Pavel Sergerov was as close as I'd ever come to meeting one. Artem, on the other hand, was a self-righteous prick.

I slid into the driver's seat, making sure he could hear the engine starting as I fired the old bird up. "Don't say you're missin' me, Art. We'll be reunited soon."

"Watch your fucking tongue." His voice lowered. "You have an hour."

The call ended.

I cursed under my breath. I *hadn't* been late, but I would be now that he'd moved our meeting up by forty-five minutes. It'd take me that long just to get out of London, never mind dump the body before getting my arse down to Arundel. Biting back another curse, I was just about to toss my phone onto the passenger seat when it vibrated again.

Fucking Artem.

"What?" I growled into the receiver.

"It's me."

Yarik.

Two little words and it felt like I'd taken a sledge-hammer to the chest. He didn't sound at all the same. 'Course, he wouldn't. He wasn't twelve anymore, shyly knocking on my door in the middle of the night, hoping to hang out even when we both knew his father would beat him black and blue for acting like I hung the moon. Petr had hated that about his son, how he used to follow me around, the hollow look in his dark blue eyes a silent confession that he was desperate for friendship, a connection, anyone that wouldn't treat him with icy cold disdain.

So, yeah, he wasn't twelve anymore. It was just that I hadn't expected to hear the rasping timbre that would probably only deepen more with time. For a second, I almost mourned the loss of the kid I once knew, the boy who sat on top of a closed suitcase and dared me to uncover all his secrets.

I'd known that Yarik like the back of my hand.

I knew this one, too, through the texts we sent back and forth. But it was one thing to read his words on a screen and something else entirely to hear this new soft rasp in my ear. It was . . . unnerving, to say the least. What else didn't I know about my best mate?

"Kirill? You there?"

My name was laced with a hint of anxiety he couldn't hide, and it took me ten solid seconds to realize that even though I was driving on autopilot, my body knowing exactly where it had to go, I still hadn't said a word. Clearing my throat, I tried for a smile, hoping he'd hear it in my voice. "Sorry, yeah. Been a long day."

"Might end up being a little bit longer."

That got my attention. "What did you do?"

He tried for a laugh, but it came out sounding all wrong. "What makes you think I did something?"

"Yarik."

"Kiryusha."

At the Russian pet name for Kirill that only he ever used, I rolled my eyes. "Don't even try."

"You're no fun."

"So you've told me a hundred times."

"A hundred?" There was a real laugh. No longer soft, but gruff, as if it came from the beating heart of his soul. The sound scraped down my spine like a whisper of lost time. "Make that a thousand. More than that, probably. I've never met anyone as allergic to fun as you are."

"You done being a brat?"

"No."

"Yaroslav—"

"I'm here."

"What?"

"In London. Well, I'm at Heathrow but—"

My heart lurched, the organ suddenly pounding so loud, I couldn't hear anything over the deafening roar in my ears. Yarik, here in England? Here in *London*? The motorway ahead of me blurred, and I had a stray worry of driving straight into the crash belt, the car wrapped around twisted metal like an accordion, the dead body in the boot being found by the police when they arrived on scene.

Fuck.

Fuck—

"Volkov didn't mention you coming home." Don't know how I managed to get the words out past the knot in my throat, but I did, only to feel dread take its place as the silence on the other end of the line lengthened. "Yarik," I said slowly, and I wasn't the kind of bloke who begged, but there was no mistaking the edge of panic in my voice when I repeated, "He didn't mention you coming home."

Don't say it.

Please, don't say—

"He doesn't know."

Fuck.

"I was hoping you might give me a ride?"

A ride to *where*? Straight into a fucking grave? Just dump his body in alongside Jocle Stevens like he wasn't worthy of a better ending? I knew that Yarik hated Moscow. I could read between the lines to all the things he never said out loud, to the pieces of his heart that he broke off in shards, never knowing how much they made me bleed. Whether he wanted to acknowledge it or not, Moscow was better than London. For him. It was better for *him*.

Away from Petr Volkov.

Away from this life.

Away from me, even, because I hid things, too, and as much as Yarik liked to pretend that I was the same kid he'd found washed up on the banks of the River Thames, the pieces of my heart, if I ever shared them with him, would cut so deep, they'd bleed him dry.

I gripped the steering wheel hard, struggling to put words to the riot of emotions swarming my brain. Finally, I said, "I have a dead body in the boot right now."

"Oh."

Yeah, *oh*. This was the life he'd managed to escape for the past three years. The killing, the deception, the rest of it. Moscow probably wasn't a utopia, but it had to be better than the monotonous grind of being the Bratva's bitch. Although maybe being the Bratva's prince made things different. I didn't think so, but what did I know? "Artem is expecting me in Arundel in an hour. I don't know how long it'll be."

"Right." That rasp had softened to a careful whisper, and I could almost picture him now, standing in front of the airport, his arms wrapped tight around his chest as he watched families come and go out of Heathrow while he stood alone. "No worries. I'll, uh . . . I'll figure something out. I shouldn't have thought you would—I mean, I shouldn't have expected you to drop everything and—"

"I need you to find a place to camp out." The slight hitch in his breathing told me that I'd startled him a little. Good. He gave me the shock of a lifetime ringing me out of the blue on a bloody Tuesday evening, ready to turn my world upside down all over again. "If I don't show up, Artem will be the least of my problems. Yours, too."

Maybe he could read between the lines as well as I could because he didn't argue with me, just said, "I know, I'm sorry," like his showing up was only a massive inconvenience and not the one move on a chessboard that could send his father spiraling out with rage.

Or maybe he did know.

That was the thing about Yarik; he was impulsive, but he was razor-sharp, too—the kind of smart that would one day raze whole cities to the ground if anyone dared to get in his way. He was sly and quick-witted, stubborn as hell, and—

"I need you to stay out of sight. I'll text you when I get close—tell you where to meet me."

He released a soft sigh, and it sounded like relief. "Okay."

"I mean it, Yarik. Out of sight."

"Boo," he quipped, and it was so like him to say something so randomly ridiculous, that I didn't know whether to laugh or tell him to piss off. "Like a ghost, I got it, Kiryusha. Now you see me, now you don't."

I cracked a smile. A real one, this time. I wondered if he could tell, if he could hear it when I said, "I've got to go; I'll see you soon," as if my hands weren't sweating on the steering wheel and my heart wasn't racing with the near-forgotten thrill of doing something that I knew could get me killed but I'd do it anyway because there wasn't anything I wouldn't do for Yaroslav Volkov even if it meant saving him from himself.

Before I could hang up, he said, "Hey, Kirill?"

"Yeah?"

"I missed you."

And then he ended the call.

By the time I got to Heathrow, it was after one in the morning.

The place was eerily empty, the night sky still but for the heavy clouds that misted over the city and blocked out the stars. And then there was Yarik, striding toward me with his shoulders thrown back as if he had no reason at all to hide, his blond hair illuminated to a pale-gold sheen under the lampposts.

I wanted to throttle him.

I also wanted to drag him into my car and never let him out of my sight again.

I was out the door in the next second, moving before my brain could catch up with my muscles, my limbs, which were already putting me on a direct path to my best friend. He met my gaze in the last second before I crowded close and pulled him in for a hug that I hated as much as I craved. He must have sensed my internal struggle, though, because he stood there like a life-sized doll, arms limp where they rested down at his sides, his body quivering but held unnaturally still—except for the shallow puff of air against my neck that told me he was alive, that he was giving me this moment, even when it went against every part of his nature not to throw his arms around me and hug me back.

My skin felt tight.

My heart was pounding, thrashing, within its cage.

Then I was stepping back and letting the brisk autumn air rush in between us, whisking away the rare display of affection like it never happened at all. I turned away before he could see the reel of emotion play out across my face, but red-hot embarrassment still dogged my heels as I gestured to the car. "Come on. Let's get out of here." We'd tempted fate by staying too long as it was.

He tossed his rucksack into the backseat, then got in the front with me. "Are we going to talk about that? I think we should."

"No."

"You hugged me."

I bit the inside of my cheek. "A temporary lapse in judgment."

"You *missed* me."

With one hand on the steering wheel, I glanced at him out of the corner of my eye, only to find him sitting in the passenger seat with his hands tucked beneath his chin while he batted his eyelashes at me like his life depended on it. I tried to look away, back to the road, but he caught on to the aversion tactic too quick. Suddenly, he was swaying his whole body forward, pose still going strong, so that he could stay in my line of vision.

"You missed me," he pressed in a sing-song lilt that should have grated my nerves but only made me bite my cheek harder, this time against a smile. "Admit it. You. Missed. Me."

"Yarik—"

"It could be my last night, you know."

It could. We both knew it. Still, I rolled my eyes just to mess with him. "That'd be unfortunate."

"*Unfortunate*? I could die tomorrow, and that's all you have to say? You'd be wracked with guilt for the rest of your life."

"Would I?"

"*Yes.*"

"Good to know all the indigestion will have a root cause."

Stagnant silence landed between us for only a second before it was devoured by the sound of laughter—mine, his, ours. It bubbled up in a way that I'd forgotten it could, warm and unbridled. I only ever laughed like this with him. It burned my chest. Heartburn. A medical condition without a cure, and even if it had one, I still wouldn't choose to numb the pain. It felt too good.

"Fucking wanker," he muttered, but the smirk riding his lips said that he didn't really mean it, and I cared about him enough to make myself confess, "Sometimes I missed you."

You know, if "sometimes" was just a less pathetic way of saying, "I missed you every second of every day."

Which was true.

I'd missed him every second of every day of every year that he'd been gone.

"I'm assuming you have a plan?" I asked as I pulled away from the curb. When he didn't answer right away, I spared him a quick glance. "Yarik. A plan. Tell me you have one."

"Sort of."

Sort of. Fucking hell.

If I weren't keen on keeping us alive, I'd have closed

my eyes, just out of frustration. As it was, I stared out at the spot-lit road ahead of us and counted to ten. Not that it helped much. "You're telling me that you hopped on a plane without—" Hold on. My gaze cut to his profile again. "How did you afford the fare?"

He visibly squirmed. "About that..."

We hadn't even left Heathrow yet, but that didn't matter. I pulled over, cut the engine, and turned to stare at the kid in the passenger seat. Because maybe he wasn't twelve anymore, but he was still that—still just a *kid*. Older, sure, and physically bigger, definitely, but the same boy who made reckless decisions left and right, the kind that always got him backed into a corner with no way out.

No way out aside from *me*, that was.

"Was I your plan?" I bit out the question before it had even fully formed. "And don't lie. I'll see right through it."

As he fiddled with the drawstring on his black hoodie, I was struck with the sudden visual of him slipping through the streets of Moscow with that hood drawn up over his head, hoping that his father's spies wouldn't catch sight of him as he made his way to the airport on his own. A mafia prince on the run. It could almost be the start of a bad joke except that there was nothing funny about what Petr would do to his only son the moment he found out that Yarik was back on British soil, uninvited.

"Yaroslav..."

"I know what you're thinking." There was a vehemence to his voice that I hadn't expected. "That I'm selfish—"

I'd thought a lot of things about him over the years, but that had never been one of them. Selfish implied that he thought of no one but himself. That he would always put his own wants and needs first, fuck everyone else. Yarik wasn't selfish. He was the furthest thing from it. I opened my mouth to tell him that, except he was already on a roll, his dark blue eyes flashing with so much ire, I felt scorched alive.

"—Like some pampered little prince who can do whatever he wants, whenever he wants." He slung an arm around the headrest of his seat, but it was only so he could thrust his face close to mine without needing to use the center console or my thigh for balance. Even now, with him spitting fire the way he was, he was still so careful not to touch me, to keep his distance, however he could. "The prince decides to come home on a whim," he added, lashes fluttering fast, not teasing this time, but like he was desperate to keep his walls from crumbling. "The prince decides to leave everything behind just because he's *bored*."

He was unraveling before me.

I could see it—could feel the electric current in the air, the way he was hovering on the precipice of something dark and turbulent.

"Maybe I *was* bored," he sneered. "Maybe I did come home on a whim. Maybe this has nothing to do with *you*."

"You weren't bored."

"You don't know that."

"And this wasn't some *whim*," I said, talking right over him. "I told you not to lie to me, that I'd see right through it."

There was just enough light in the car for me to see what my words did to him. His shoulders shuddered and his expression fractured and before I could stop him, he threw open his door and clambered out of the passenger seat.

I followed him.

There wasn't any other option.

It didn't matter that we hadn't breathed the same air in close to three years. We were bound, the two of us, and if I had to chase him down, just to keep him from doing something irreversibly stupid, I would. A million times over, I would.

"Yarik!" I shouted into the wind. "Yarik, stop."

He didn't stop. He was walking fast with his head down and his hood up. I rushed to catch up to him. Instead of laying a hand on him when I got close, I threw myself directly in his way. Even now, he was taller than I was. He probably always would be. But I'd started to fill out in every other regard, and if he planned to bowl me over to keep on running, he'd have a harder time now than he would have when we'd first met.

We were both breathing fast and not from the exertion. Beneath the fabric of his hood, I could see indecision play out across his features. When he fell back a step, his shoulders already twisting in retreat, I growled, "Don't run away from me."

Still, he stepped back.

I immediately closed the gap. "Don't."

"Kirill—"

"You know what selfish is?" I was stalking him now, closing in as he fell back step after step. "Selfish is pretending I don't give a fuck about you when you know that's not true. Selfish is acting like I don't understand when you won't tell me what's going on. *Selfish*, Yaroslav, is running the fuck away instead of asking me to fix the problem."

The wind tore his hood down.

It left him exposed.

To the elements, to my gaze, to the truth that I'd thrown down at his feet.

He backed up another step, but I'd cornered him right up against my car, exactly where he'd tried to flee. He looked shell-shocked. Or maybe it wasn't shock so much as it was fear. But it couldn't be me that he was afraid of, so what had made him react like this? What had put him on an airplane without his father's blessing, prepared to step into the lion's den instead of staying far away where he was better off?

I stepped right up to him. Mere centimeters separated my chest from his. Though my nerves clawed at me to put more space between us, I held my ground and stayed right where I was. "You gonna say something to that?" It was a taunt as much as it was a plea. I'd dangle him right over the edge of a cliff if I had to, but I'd pull him back long before I ever let him drop into the churning sea. "Tell me I'm wrong. Tell me you aren't a selfish little brat, thinking you know better than everyone else."

"Shut up." The demand tremored in the wind. "Just *shut up*."

"Why?"

"What do you mean, *why*?"

"You have something to say, then say it. Tell. Me. I'm. Wrong."

"I couldn't stay!" Part of me thought he shouted it, but maybe that wasn't right. Maybe it only felt that way because he said it with every fiber of his being, as if he'd screamed the words into the void a thousand times before, only for them to never be heard. "Are you happy now?" Breathing hard, he scrubbed the heel of his palm across his face. Too late, I realized that he was crying. "I couldn't stay."

The way his voice cracked . . . "Yarik, talk to me. *Please.*"

Frantically, he shook his head.

"You were fine," I said, but even as I did, I wondered if that was true. Over the years, I'd suspected that something was wrong. Yarik had a way about him; he could throw off a scent with the best of them, always skirting around topics that made him jumpy. But that didn't make him impossible to read, and just because he could radiate sunshine didn't mean that he wasn't also cloaked in shadows. "Please. Just say *something.*"

"It wasn't safe."

I felt my entire body go rigid. "Someone put their hands on you." It wasn't a question, and neither were the thoughts tumbling through my head. Someone had hurt him. Or threatened to, at least. That was enough to make me see red. "Who?" I bit out. "One of your guards? The Zharkov—"

Yarik slid out from between me and the vehicle. "No."

"You said that it wasn't safe." I didn't chase after him, but he also wasn't trying to run. He paced in front of me, back and forth, his fingers clawing at his hair like he fought demons no one saw but him. Down at my sides, my own fingers curled into fists. "Give me a name."

"I don't have a name."

"But you—"

"It wasn't safe for *me*, okay? No one touched me. No one hurt me."

"I don't understand."

He spun around so suddenly, I experienced whiplash. There was something in his stance that felt . . . fragile. Glass threaded through with hairline fractures. Maybe the crack had always been there, only made obvious thanks to us reuniting after years apart, or maybe it was new. Like he hadn't yet adjusted to existing in skin that no longer fit him. There was a slump to his shoulders, a tremble in his fingertips, just before he hid them in the front pocket of his hoodie.

I didn't like it.

It all felt wrong.

I have loads of secrets, he once told me. I hadn't believed him then, but I believed him now.

Softly, he said, "I know you don't."

Understand, he meant. He knew that I didn't understand.

Instead of bothering to explain, he muttered, "C'mon, we need to go," and then he got in the car without another word.

There was a strange, hollow feeling in my chest that told me I'd missed something big just now, and that I wouldn't get this moment back. But when I sat in the driver's seat and turned to look at him, it was clear that the conversation was over. He'd thrown his hoodie back up and curled his big frame against the door, huddled as far away from me as possible.

Confused, I rasped out his name.

"It's okay, Kiryusha." He smiled, but it was a brittle, tragic thing. "And you're right, as usual. I didn't have a plan." His low chuckle was grim. "I guess I just wanted to see you before he found out that I was back, and you need to fake-hate me again for the rest of our lives."

"For the rest of our lives is a really, really long time."

Even saying it out loud had my lungs seizing tight. Yaroslav Volkov was my best friend, the only family I had. More than a thousand text messages between us proved that there wasn't anything I wouldn't do for him. He'd reached for the stars in Moscow, and I'd scoured the skies for them here in London. I needed him to be okay.

"Maybe." He offered me a small shrug that I didn't believe for a second. "But with how I expect Father to react to me coming home, you'll only have to fake-hate me for, oh, probably another twenty-four hours."

I stared at him, wishing he would meet my gaze. "I worry that you'll regret coming back."

He looked out the window, his profile silhouetted by a streak of moonlight. "I won't," he said solemnly. "I promise you, I won't."

CHAPTER THIRTEEN
YARIK

I didn't regret anything.

PART FOUR
LONDON, ENGLAND

CHAPTER FOURTEEN

KIRILL

The Volkov family was at war.

You'd never know it just by looking at them—because not even Nina, whom everyone knew was prone to dramatics, would dare do something as stupid as embarrass her father in front of his guests—but there was no denying the obvious: they were all poised to make the killing blow.

Petr, specifically.

Seated like a king at the head of the table, he made a point to chat amiably with Enzo Accardi, but every time the Italian don paused the conversation to funnel another bite of golubsty into his mouth, Volkov's gaze shot down the length of the table to glare daggers at his son. And Yarik . . . Fuck, I wanted nothing more than to grab him by the shoulders and shake some sense into his thick, stubborn skull, because it was obvious to everyone, except maybe Enzo Accardi, that Yarik didn't give two shits about why the Accardi family had been invited from Italy to celebrate his eighteenth birthday.

Seated across from Yarik was the *why*.

Her name was Giulia. She was nineteen, fluent in both Italian and English, and was currently studying art history at Oxford. *A temporary pastime,* Accardi had boasted with a careless smile when we'd first sat down to eat, *before marriage and babies, of course.*

Of course.

If Giulia harbored any resentment toward her father about her uni days coming to a swift end, she didn't show it. She smiled and laughed and tried to make eye contact with Yarik, who looked absolutely miserable sandwiched between Nina and Vera, and whose gaze constantly sought out mine instead.

I'd been placed at the end of the table.

With Artem.

"More yorsh, Volkov." He didn't bother to look me in the eye—just waved a hand at his empty glass. He might as well have snapped his fingers at me. My jaw went tight, vision bloomed red, right there at the edges where my morals tended to lie in ruin, and it took every scrap of self-control I possessed not to reach out and break that hand in half.

I was tired.

Tired of obeying.

Tired of always keeping my mouth shut.

"Volkov." Artem's tone roughened with warning. "More yorsh."

Fuck you.

Fuck you.

Fuck you—

Inwardly, I choked on a rage so hot, I was surprised that I didn't burn alive. Outwardly, I calmly pushed my chair back, picked up the empty glass, and forced an expression of apathy onto my face as I approached the sideboard to do the honors of making Volkov's newly promoted councilor a bloody fucking drink. Vodka. Beer. I grabbed the appropriate bottles, sorely tempted to search the house from top to bottom for some arsenic, and then poured equal measures of both into the glass. Sans arsenic.

Unfortunately.

Just as I turned to retake my seat, Enzo Accardi said, "Tell me, Kirill. All these years and you were never able to reconnect with your family?"

The question stopped me in my tracks.

This wasn't my first time meeting Accardi. He visited England frequently, and just last year, I'd escorted Volkov to the Accardi family villa in Sorrento. While the bosses had talked business into the late-night hours, Artem had made me play chauffeur, driving him to an old, decaying mansion buried in the Amalfi cliffside. Wasn't sure what I'd expected, honestly, but it hadn't been the woman who'd greeted him at the door, then beckoned him inside with her fingers tucked into his belt loops and a come-hither smile on her lips. We hadn't made it back to Sorrento until after four in the morning.

Point was, Accardi knew me. Maybe not well, because at events like these, I did my best to fade into the wallpaper, as any good soldier would do, but well enough. So, why ask about my family now?

My gaze slid to Volkov, who watched me with a predatory stillness that set off alarm bells in my head. Loud ones. Was this a trick? Some sort of trap to test my allegiance, yet again? My pulse tripped over itself even as I answered, "No, *signore.*"

"Not for a lack of trying, though."

Fucking Vera.

Yarik's cousin met my gaze with a vicious twist of her lips. "Remember that time you went through Dyadya Petr's study?" She flicked a glance to her uncle, and then flicked her long, brown hair over one shoulder. "You tried so hard to find any information on—"

"*Shut up*," hissed Yarik.

I was frozen, feet cemented to the floor while my heart rabbited in my chest. Loyalty was everything in the Bratva. And Vera had just outed me over something I'd done years ago when I was still new to this world and didn't know how fast a bullet traveled or how easy it was to pull a trigger. Or, you know, the fact that security cameras existed, and Petr Volkov was a paranoid madman who left nothing to chance.

Christ. I didn't want to die, and she'd just sealed my fate.

"What?" Vera prompted, baiting me like the hellhound she was. "Nothing to say to that?"

"Igor."

Halfway down the table, the younger Volkov startled at the sound of his older brother's voice. Not just his brother—his *pakhan*. All around, wide-eyed stares volleyed from one Volkov to the other, until finally Igor lowered his silverware to the table, a piece of red meat still caught in the fork tines. Dread seemed to weight his every movement as he rubbed a hand over his bearded jaw. "*Da*."

Petr didn't even blink. In Russian, he said, "Until your daughter understands how she should conduct herself at a formal gathering, she's not welcome at this table."

"*Konoshno*," Igor said flatly. He pushed his chair back. "Vera, let's go."

And that was that.

Vera was older than me, and maybe growing up meant maturity for other people, but she was hostile. Always had been, even when we'd been kids. She reminded me of Volkov's dogs, jerking at their chains, biting anyone who stepped too close. Loyal to no one, not even the hand that fed them. So, while her outburst wasn't exactly surprising, it still threw me that she'd kept this information to herself for over eight years, just to . . . what, drop it on me now? For what reason?

With a roll of her eyes, Vera tossed her napkin across her unfinished dinner, then sauntered out of the dining room ahead of her father. In the awkward lull that followed, I braced myself for the impending storm.

Volkov would have my head for this. And if not my head, then definitely my—

"My apologies," he said, wine bottle in hand so that he could refill Enzo's glass with a red blend from Accardi's own vineyards. "One would think that as our children age, we are able to loosen their collars. Give them more breathing room." The smile that stretched across his face didn't meet the wintry steel of his cold blue eyes. "But that would be a mistake, of course. Our children are spoiled, too soft to endure what we did in our youth, no?"

Accardi took the proffered wine. Briefly, his stare touched upon his daughter, who'd fallen silent like the rest of us, before he brought the glass to his lips. After a healthy swallow, he returned it to the table. Danced his fingers along the crystal stem. "All the more reason to give them a guiding hand."

Petr raised his glass almost mockingly. "As I've said."

"You have. Repeatedly."

"And you've made your feelings known, too. Unless . . . have they changed?"

Accardi's dark brown eyes swept back over his daughter, then Yarik, where they lingered long enough to raise the hair on the back of my neck. I found myself taking a step in Yaroslav's direction just as the don murmured, "Yes."

Victory flashed in Petr's narrowed gaze. "Say it, then."

"Yes, I—" Another quick, resolute glance aimed at his daughter. "I agree to the terms of the marriage contract for my Giulia and your son."

There was absolute stillness.

And then—

"Marriage contract?" Yarik's voice wavered with horror as he looked from Accardi to Giulia to his father. "And what do you mean, *terms*?" Before Volkov could answer, Yarik launched out of his seat, knocking his wine glass over in the process. It spilled across the table, staining the white linen a deep, ambushed red. "I didn't sign anything. Father, you can't just—"

"Sit down."

"No."

"I said, *sit down*."

Yarik didn't sit, and I didn't know whether to grab him by the shoulder and force him down into the chair or move in front of him, an impregnable fortress that would absorb each and every blow even if it meant putting myself in the line of fire instead. Then I realized that I was still holding Artem's yorsh, the request for it forgotten as everyone's attention shifted to my best friend.

"I'm not going to *marry her*," he was protesting loudly. "I don't care if you've signed a hundred contracts —a-a thousand, even. You promised that I'd have a choice. That you wouldn't make me—"

"I lied."

The temperature in the room dropped to below freezing. No one moved. No one breathed. Least of all me. Least of all *Yarik.*

"You, what." It wasn't a question. A flush stained my best mate's cheeks. Down by his sides, his arms twitched, as if he wanted to wrap them around himself. Or like he wanted to deck his father right in the face, consequences be damned.

"I lied." Volkov coolly sipped his wine. "I will forgive this outburst, *syn*, as I'm sure you're in shock. But let me make myself very clear—you have no choice in the matter."

"No." A whisper. A breath.

The rhythm of my heart matched the panic flooding Yarik's face while waves of nausea pooled in my gut, the likes of which I hadn't felt in years. Not since Pavel Sergerov. Not since I'd *killed* Pavel Sergerov.

Petr continued, unbothered. "This is the way of things. You marry. You give the family heirs. One day when I'm dead, you'll assume my place and rule my kingdom. Then your children will marry. And they will give the family heirs. So on, so forth, for eternity." He tipped back the rest of his wine. "Enzo, tell me, *pozhaluysta*. Does your daughter give you such grief?"

Accardi laughed, but the sound lagged, hitting a beat too late to come off as anything but strained. "Giulia? No, my Giulia knows her place."

Giulia said nothing.

"Perhaps I shall remind my son of his place." Volkov snagged the wine bottle and poured, and poured, and poured until red liquid kissed the rim. He wasn't drunk. That wasn't his way. He liked to draw out the inevitable, crafting silk webs around his prey until they either suffocated or he cut them loose in a rare show of mercy. "Or perhaps," he added in a deadly soft murmur, "I will have his best friend remind him as penance for invading my privacy."

Slowly, like a doll in a horror film, Nina's head turned my way.

So did Artem's.

Condensation from the yorsh coated my palm, but it was nothing compared to the nervous perspiration beading to life on my brow. Anxiety gathered in my throat until it hurt to even swallow.

I wasn't stupid. No way would Volkov let a bomb like the one Vera dropped go unpunished. Maybe that made me naïve, though, because I hadn't expected *this* to be his power move. Based on the way his gaze glittered with satisfaction, he knew that he had me backed into a corner.

No one spoke out against Petr Volkov.

He was the *pakhan*.

Our king.

Over the years, I'd watched him break those around me. He seemed to relish that final moment, when his victims dropped to their knees and begged for their lives. Worse was when they begged not for themselves, but their loved ones—*please hurt me instead, please don't touch my wife, my children, my family*. There weren't any lines Volkov wouldn't cross, especially if he felt personally slighted.

And now he wanted . . . Now, he wanted *me* to . . .

"Enzo, Giulia." Volkov rose to his full height, dabbed his mouth with the napkin, and discarded it on the table beside his plate. "You'll have to excuse us."

Accardi didn't move a muscle. "*Sì, naturalmente.* Tomorrow, then."

"Tomorrow," Volkov returned.

He walked out.

And we followed, Yarik and me. Forever bound. Even in Hell.

CHAPTER FIFTEEN

KIRILL

Volkov's study was eerily quiet as he closed the door behind us. Or maybe it only felt that way to me.

I was dimly aware of father and son arguing, but I couldn't focus on anything but how time seemed to have crawled to a standstill. In my periphery, Volkov moved to stand beside his desk with Yarik nipping at his heels, his hands gesturing wildly in the moonlight. The latter slanted through parted drapes and illuminated the otherwise dark room. It washed over me, too. Made it impossible to hide in the shadows the way I had for years now.

I wouldn't let this happen.

I *couldn't*—

Volkov was still going off, saying what, I didn't know. No matter how hard I tried to break through the chains of panic, I felt stuck, paralyzed, unable to draw even the slightest bit of oxygen into my screaming lungs. Time trudged on—left me locked inside that old warehouse in Moscow, my clothes, hands, hair all covered in death. It didn't matter that I'd scrubbed myself raw after—the betrayal still stained my soul.

And now my boss wanted me to . . .

On a ragged breath, I squeezed my eyes shut. No. No way would I ever hurt Yarik the way I'd hurt Sergerov. Not to teach him a lesson. Not even to save my own life. Fuck that.

Yarik was shouting. His panic was the only thing that could supersede my own, and I fumbled with the Bad Things Box inside my head, cracking open the heavy lid and shoving a dead Pavel Sergerov back inside where he belonged. Shoved all my fear in there, too, because I couldn't watch Yarik's back if I was too busy watching my own.

"I'm not doing it," he told Volkov fiercely. "Go ahead and ambush me like you did at dinner every day for the rest of my life—doesn't matter to me. I'm not marrying Giulia Accardi. I'm not marrying *anyone*."

Petr's nostrils flared. "You have a duty to this family."

"I don't care."

"You should."

"Why? Because you need more heirs to continue this trainwreck of a family? Because this is what the Bratva does?" Like the impulsive fool he'd been since childhood, Yarik didn't bend—or break. Just lifted his chin and stared his father down. "I don't need the Bratva. I don't need *you*."

"But he does."

You'd think that with all the strict firearm laws in the UK, it'd be impossible to get away with running an entire criminal enterprise based on manufacturing and selling weapons, but the rules never seemed to apply to Volkov or to his family. And I wasn't a member of the family.

The gun Volkov pulled out and aimed at my face hammered that point home for good.

I dragged in a shaky, uneven breath.

"I brought him into this house because you begged me." Volkov didn't look my way, the whole of his attention rooted on his son. "I gave him structure. I gave him purpose. And while you, my own flesh and blood, might think that you are better off without me, Kirill here knows that isn't true for himself. Without me, he would be no one. Nameless. Alone in the world. Rubbish tossed aside, unwanted."

Unwanted.

My chest burned. My fingers curled—but there was nothing to hold onto. Nothing tangible, anyway. Just the familiar gut punch of agony. For all his faults, Volkov wasn't lying, not about me. I was no one without the Bratva. Nameless. Alone in the world. Rubbish tossed aside, unwanted by the same people—whoever they were—who should have loved me unconditionally.

I was the boy who'd washed up on the River Thames.

Some part of me was *still* that boy, stupid and endlessly naïve, despite the fact that it hadn't taken me all that long to accept that my entire existence was apparently forgettable. No one had searched for me. No one had hunted me down, feverish with worry that I might be forever lost to them. Even paying for bloodwork recently had, to the geneticist's surprise, revealed no trace of a family who might claim me as their own. I'd learned that I was Irish and Japanese. Beyond that, I could have been anyone.

My throat closed up as the ugly truth seeped into my bones.

I was *unwanted*.

"I can kill him just as easily as I can let him live," Volkov told his son without even a trace of inflection. "The choice is yours."

Yarik glanced at me. Hope burned in his gaze. "We can leave. Right now, I mean. Just walk out and never look back."

We'd be killed before we even reached the property line. Hadn't he warned me of that when we were kids? And maybe it was selfish of me, but I'd rather him be alive and miserable than happy and dead. Dead was permanent. Dead was forever. Dead wasn't an option.

I turned to my *pakhan*. "Punish me instead."

"Kirill," Yarik burst out, "no. Don't—"

"You're angry that Yaroslav embarrassed you in front of Accardi. And you're angry with me, too, because we both know that I spent years going behind your back every chance I got, always looking for a way out. You're offended by my presence. That I spat on your hospitality. It doesn't matter that I've done everything you've asked for the better part of five years. Judgment has already been passed, and I failed. Am I right?"

Those cold blue eyes turned glacial. "*Da.*"

"Then take it out on me."

"No." A hand wrapped around my bicep and tugged me backward, putting me behind a body larger than my own but still lanky with youth. I managed to right my equilibrium and lunge forward, putting us shoulder-to-shoulder, just as Yarik growled, "*Don't touch him.*"

For a moment, Volkov only stared at his son.

And then he cut him down, the way only he could, right there at the knees: "The irony, Yaroslav, that you'd risk your own life to protect someone who has been a better son to me, and to this family, than you ever have."

Before either of us could recover from that emotional blow, he stepped close and pressed the gun to Yarik's temple. "Shirt, off. Then get the rope."

All color drained from my best friend's face.

What did that mean, get the rope? Why was—?

Like he couldn't bear the thought of my eyes on him, Yarik twisted away. Wordlessly, he ripped the tails of his dress shirt from his waistband before attacking the buttons with what I could only imagine were trembling fingers. Even his shoulders trembled. Meanwhile, Volkov never lowered the gun from his son's head.

At Volkov's dinner table, no one was allowed a firearm aside from the *pakhan*. His rule. One that we all made sure to obey. Not a problem, usually, but that meant I was currently unarmed. If I stepped out of line, Petr would pull the trigger. Even if he didn't, I'd bet that his bodyguards were already in the hall, just waiting for the signal to bust down the door.

We'd be dead in a heartbeat, me and Yarik.

No do-overs.

No second chances.

The fucking end.

With my heart pounding erratically, I watched Yarik shrug out of his shirt and toss it aside. It fluttered to the floor like a white flag of surrender. I couldn't say the last time that I'd seen my best friend shirtless, if I ever had at all. Our world was one of death and violence; in battle, you never removed your armor.

Until now.

Shimmering moonlight ghosted over his pale white skin, revealing a web of textured scarring that criss-crossed over the broad expanse of his back. There were hundreds. Too many to count. Where the scars overlapped, the flesh was thick and almost grotesquely uneven, a sharp contrast to the thin, spidery lines hidden like wraiths near his waist.

His back was a map of horrors.

Horrors that rippled with the movement of his arm, and it was only then that I tore my gaze away long enough to see him reach for a length of rope that hung from a silver hook on the wall. Immediately, I zeroed in on the messy patchwork of paint beneath it. As if . . . as if the hook had been adjusted over the years to match the height of a growing boy.

I swayed on my feet.

I might have said his name then, whispered it, even, but when Yarik turned back around, he kept his gaze fixed on the floor. It was, I thought with a surge of terror, the first time in all the years I'd known him that he'd actively avoided making eye contact with me.

With his head bowed, he handed the rope to his father, who—

No.

No bloody way.

"You asked me to punish you instead," Volkov said as I physically recoiled from his outstretched hand. "So, I will. This is to be your punishment."

The terror in my blood sprouted wings of fury. "Kill me, then. Because I won't—"

"Stand your ground, and I'll pull the trigger."

"You wouldn't." My mouth went bone dry as I shot a startled glance toward Yarik. "You said it yourself—he's your heir."

"I have another."

Wait. He couldn't mean . . . "*Nina?*"

"There'd be pushback, I'm sure. A girl in charge?" He

huffed out a humorless laugh. "But maybe it's time for a change, especially if my own son can't handle the responsibilities that come with his position. If that's the case, then I'm only expediting the future because no one will respect a *pakhan* who puts himself above his men." His finger settled on the trigger. "Take the rope, Kirill, for his sake, if not your own. I won't tell you again."

There was no love lost between father and son. Everyone knew they hated each other, but I hadn't thought it would ever get this far—that Petr Volkov would rather murder his own kid than let him stand on his own two feet away from the Bratva and its old-school expectations.

Stupid. Endlessly naïve. Because I *should* have known.

Volkov was a coldblooded monster; he'd destroy his own family without a second thought and then make up for the loss by marrying someone else, knocking her up, and producing a second batch of offspring. Or a third. Or however long it took him to populate his line with a string of obedient heirs. Heirs like picture-perfect Giulia Accardi who knew her place.

Yarik rasped out my name.

It was my turn to avoid his gaze. My turn to reach for the rope and wrap its length around my fist. I had a momentary, impossible fantasy of using it as a noose on Volkov, but even if I managed to pull it off, we'd never get past the guards at the door. The window wasn't an option, either, not when the study was on the second floor.

Better alive and miserable than happy and dead.

"Against the wall." My voice was low, rough with purpose. I hadn't cried in years, but I would now if I let myself. Already, I could feel tears burning the backs of my eyes. When Yarik didn't move, I felt myself crack in two. "Fucking *now*, Yaroslav."

I put my hand on his back, right over all those old scars, and pushed him toward the wall. He stumbled. Peered back at me with a bewildered look on his face like he wasn't sure how he'd found himself in the middle of a waking nightmare and didn't know how to get himself out of it.

We were both in that nightmare.

Both drowning. Both screaming to *wake up, wake up, wake up.*

Tremors shook me to my core as I cut my gaze away and used my body to corner his. He was bigger than me, had always been bigger than me, and it said a lot about his current state of mind that he let me push him around, backing him up against the wall until the only way out was through me. The air between us crackled with renewed tension, and still, I couldn't bring myself to look at him, not even when I grabbed his wrists, looped the rope around them both, and cinched the knot tight.

He said my name again. Panicked. Desperate.

I didn't need to see his expression to know what he wanted, which fate he'd prefer.

"No." My soul screamed the word even though it fell as a whisper from my lips. "No, Yarik."

"Kiryusha, please."

"*No,*" I snarled. *I won't let you go.*

Better alive and miserable than happy and dead.

Wrapping a hand around his linked wrists, I dragged them above his head and looped the rope over the hook. The same place where he'd been beaten by his monster of a father for fuck knows how long. The same place where I was about to . . .

"Don't move," I warned shakily.

He ducked his head, forcing me finally to look him in the eye. I hated him for it. Hated myself even more because I looked, and I looked, and I couldn't tear my gaze away, no matter how hard I tried. This was my penance. My punishment. Holding his stormy blue gaze, knowing that I was about to ruin him—ruin *us*—

Because *I* was the selfish one.

If Yarik was gone, then I'd truly be alone. I couldn't let that happen even if that meant he hated me for the rest of our lives.

I took a step back.

And then I took another and another.

Each one widened the gap between us, taking me farther away. It felt like a new beginning, but one where the storybook starts on the second page because the first has been torn out. There was a past there, an origin, but it was lost, destined to be forgotten. From this day forward, this moment would always exist between us, and our lives would be forever rewritten.

There was Before. There was After.

My heart lay shattered somewhere in between.

Volkov said, "Your belt," and that was all the direction I needed. With slow, shaking fingers, I unbuckled my belt and slid the leather through the loops of my black trousers. I did everything I could to ignore the way Yarik kept looking back at me with quick, hopeful glances like he was waiting for me to shout, "Gotcha!" as if this was some sort of awful joke.

But when I gripped the leather tighter and told him to face the wall, harsh reality stole across his features in a windfall of shock and fury and complete, utter betrayal. Something crumbled inside him, then. I saw it clear as day as though the moon weren't the one to bear witness to my selfishness but the sun instead in all its bright, burning glory.

Shoulders collapsing, Yarik turned away. Presented me with all those scars.

All that horror.

I was sick to my stomach. Any second now, what little I'd had to eat at dinner was going to come right back up. Then a noise came from outside the study, a reminder, as if I really needed one, that we weren't alone. Might never be alone again if Yarik hated me as much as I knew he would after we were done.

Better alive and miserable than happy and dead.

"We'll start with twenty," Volkov announced, "and then we'll go from there."

The study was as silent as a graveyard. I could feel my pulse hammering away. Could hear Yarik's shallow panting. Behind me, a creak of a floorboard indicated Volkov moving, and then there was pressure at the back of my skull. I didn't need to look to know what he'd done. He had me at gunpoint.

"Stop procrastinating," he warned.

I would never forgive myself for this. And Yarik would never forgive me either.

I struck him.

Once. Twice. Thrice.

He shot up onto the tips of his toes, trying to angle himself away from the crack of the belt, but even so, he didn't make a sound. Not a whimper. Not a cry. He took every lashing, withstood all the pain, as though he'd rather die than give his father the satisfaction of knowing that he'd won.

By the time we reached twenty, Volkov was seething with rage.

"Another ten," he snapped furiously, but thirty lashes didn't break his son.

Neither did forty.

Or fifty.

His legs gave out at fifty-two, the rope snapping taut as Yarik slumped over. Like a marionette doll with snipped strings, his head lolled forward on his shoulders and his knees thumped against the wall, the dead weight of his body swaying under his restrained wrists. He didn't make a sound.

I stumbled backward, my dominant arm falling limp against my side. Panting, my lips parted but nothing came out.

I did this—

—To you.

Oh, fuck. Yarik, I did this to you.

Seeing all that chaotic brilliance burned down to the wick? There was a scream inside my chest. A silent, anguished roar that I wrangled into submission long enough to bite off, "He's done."

"*Nyet.* He's done when I say he is done." Volkov snatched the belt away as if he meant to continue, and I threw myself in his path. He searched my face for half a second, looking for God knows what, and then he spat at my feet like I was an embarrassment to him. "Move aside. Now."

"He's *done*," I growled.

Volkov's blue eyes glittered dangerously. "You are walking a very fine line, Kirill."

"Then kill me. Because we both know that if I step

aside, you won't stop until he's dead." I held his narrowed gaze, refusing to back down. "But what will that say to the rest of your soldiers? That their *pakhan* was so blinded by rage, he murdered his own child? What hope do they have if you won't show your own flesh and blood any mercy?"

It was stupid, playing my cards this way. Questioning a mafia boss's decisions? He'd either put a bullet in my brain or have one of his bodyguards do it for him. Either way, I clearly had a death wish—but I was in too deep to back off.

"You've built an empire. Men who would die for you. Enemies who hear your name and scatter like rats. But if you kill Yaroslav, *that* will be your legacy. No longer the great Petr Volkov but just a weak, little man who couldn't handle some teenage rebellion."

Under his heavy, scrutinizing stare, I felt terribly exposed. Like he could see all the ways that I'd willingly sacrifice myself for Yarik even though he'd spent years warning me to stay away from his son. I used to think it was because he wanted to crush any trace of boyhood worship from Yarik's soul. Now I wasn't so sure. The way he was studying me . . . like I'd managed to *please* him, of all things, made me think that I was dead wrong.

That it wasn't his own son he'd been trying to crush all along but *me*.

I thought back to Moscow when Artem had taken the bloody blade from my hand and told me to remember what happened to traitors. I thought of every single time Volkov made me sit in his study as he poked and prodded at the black hole that was my memories. Had he even wanted me to remember? Or had he been secretly over-joyed to find himself a soldier whose loyalty could be forever manipulated to suit his needs?

Without Yarik, without Pavel Sergerov, who did I have left?

No one but *him*.

My breathing turned shallow as it registered—really, truly *registered*—just how badly I'd fucked up. I'd played right into his hand. Turned my back on Yarik because I'd been blind to the truth. Every other soldier in the Volkov syndicate had a past; they bled for Petr, sure, and would certainly suffer if they crossed him, but they still had families and loved ones who owned pieces of their heart.

Volkov wanted me alone—hostile like the dogs he kept chained to his property, loyal to no one but the hand that kept them fed.

Stupid. Endlessly naïve. When would I learn? Would I ever?

Fuck, fuck, *fuck*.

I didn't know what to do or say, just stood there in a pool of moonlight as Volkov gave me a slow, delighted smile that felt like a thousand spiders crawling down my spine. "You will meet me here first thing in the morning," he said, and then he was carelessly throwing the door open hard enough that it banged against the wall. He didn't look back at Yarik on his way out, but I did.

He was all I could see.

It wasn't until I knelt by his side and gently turned his face toward my own, ready to beg for his forgiveness, that I realized two things—his face was marked by a river of silent tears, and Petr Volkov had left before he could see that his heir, the prince to his criminal empire, was unconscious.

CHAPTER SIXTEEN

YARIK

K irill. *Kirill.*

"*Kirill—*" I gasped, jerking upright.

"Easy now." Someone touched my upper arm, using just enough pressure to hold me in place where I was sprawled out, face down on my own bed. I only knew it was mine because I could smell the lingering trace of my body wash on the sheets. But the hand on my arm . . . I didn't recognize the voice *or* the touch. Was she a doctor? The devil come to finish me off? Hard to tell when I felt like death warmed over. When I didn't respond, she awkwardly added, "You'll only hurt yourself."

"'m fine." I wasn't. Not even a little bit. I drew my free arm under my chest, ready to push up onto my elbow, but the hand on my bicep didn't budge. Irritation gritted my teeth as I tried to shake her off. "Let me go."

"Please, Mr. Volkov. Just wait before you—"

Couldn't wait.

Had to find Kirill.

A low groan spilled out of me as I scraped together the last of my strength and rolled from the bed.

Oh. Oh, bloody fucking *hell*.

Red-hot pain flashed through each of my nerve endings, lighting me up like a fireworks display. Gasping, I shot out a desperate hand to cling to the nearest bedpost. Swear to God, it didn't even help. The room was *spinning*. Squeezing my eyes shut, I slumped against the post and willed myself not to throw up all over my shoes.

Hoarsely, I croaked, "Where is he?"

"Who, Mr. Volkov? Your father?"

Fuck no.

Not him.

"Kirill," I rasped as a tremor wracked my body. "Where is he?"

"Oh. Well. I haven't seen him, but I'm sure he's around here somewhere. It's almost four in the morning."

So, he'd fled like a coward.

Eight years of friendship pissed down the drain after an hour-long descent into Hell. I'd expected more, honestly. Thought I'd at least wake up to find him by my bedside, utterly distraught over what he'd done to me in Father's study. But I was alone in this room, in this bed— the kind of alone that sank into your bones and rattled your soul.

He'd left me to fucking *rot*.

I was in so much pain, bile rose like a tidal wave every time I so much as inhaled. And, sure, the constant stream of nausea should have been reason number one to do what the doctor said and take it easy. Should have, maybe, but beneath endless layers of agony, a single flame of fury danced atop a bed of dry kindling, threatening to destroy everything in its path. Did he think that I wouldn't go after him? That he'd be free of me so long as he kept out of sight?

He'd hurt me.

Betrayed me.

Looked me right in the fucking eye and acted like what I wanted meant nothing. Acted like *I* meant nothing. He'd treated me that way, all right. Tied me up, ignored my pleas, and made my bloody father proud.

"Breathe, Mr. Volkov. You're hyperventilating—"

Soft little Yaroslav. So stupid, so dumb.

So *broken*.

"I really think you ought to . . ."

Tuning her out, I took a staggering step toward the door. I had to go. Had to find Kirill, where I'd either fall to my knees before him, a pathetic wreck of a human who would forgive anything if he just told me *why*, or I'd plant my fist in his stupid, beautiful face and ask questions later.

The doc trailed after me, wringing her hands as if this was her first night on the job and she had no idea what to do with the riot of emotion pouring from me in waves. Part of me didn't even blame her for keeping her distance. For all I'd been through, I'd never felt this unhinged. I was trembling, less than five seconds away from falling on my arse, but I kept going, even when she weakly protested, "I really do think that you should—"

I didn't give two fucks what she thought.

In a blur of rage and hurt, I stumbled down the hall in search of Kirill, growing more and more incensed the longer I went without finding him. He wasn't in his room. Wasn't in the lounge, either. Against all semblance of self-preservation, I found myself pushing the study door open to peer inside its shadowy depths; I only lasted a handful of seconds before the memory of standing nose to the wall, vulnerable and blindsided, threatened to tear me apart.

"Fucking now, Yaroslav."

I wanted to scream.

Wanted to raze the world to the ground and watch it all go up in flames.

I'd spent years doing everything I could to hide the extent of my punishments from Kirill. Yeah, he'd suspected something was going on, especially when I hurt so bad, I could barely leave my bed, but still, he hadn't *known*—not about the humiliation of being told I was worthless, right before I was shown, time and time again, how truly worthless I really was; not about the mangled scars that littered my back either.

And now . . .

"Don't move."

Now he's seen me at my worst—taken *advantage* of me at my worst—and rather than own up to it, he'd turned his back on me instead.

"Face the wall."

A brisk wind rustled through my hair as I stepped out under a starry night sky. It was only when goose bumps pebbled my chest that I gained enough self-awareness to look down and realize that I wasn't wearing a shirt. Fuck him for that, too. For crawling so deep beneath my skin that even now, when I was absolutely obliterated from the betrayal he'd leveled at my feet, he could still occupy my thoughts so completely that the world around him faded to pitch-black.

Maybe it was intuition that guided me or some higher being, or the stars themselves, but my feet drew me past the gnarled oak tree with its weeping branches and then past the thick reeds that no one ever bothered to trim back. They stroked my wounded skin like a lover's caress, even as I used my forearms to beat them out of the way, until I was stepping out into the small clearing where I'd once found an almost dead boy.

My best friend.

The other half of my wretched soul.

I shouted his name, still so angry that I could choke on it. Spun around where I stood, scouring the darkness for a glimpse of—

There.

On his knees, right near the water's edge.

"Did you really think that I wouldn't come for you?" I stalked toward him with sure footsteps even as my flesh wept fresh agony. "That I wouldn't tear the Earth apart with my own two fucking hands to find you?"

He didn't say anything.

An unforgiving gust of wind tugged at his black hair, sweeping the silky strands off the back of his neck. My gaze lowered. He was still decked out in the same clothes he'd worn to my birthday dinner—black woolen trousers paired with a long-sleeved shirt I'd gotten him last year. The fact that his belt was missing had me seeing red.

"What, nothing to say?"

He didn't look back at me. Didn't even *acknowledge* me. It was a dagger to an already bleeding heart, and I wasn't proud of it, the way I threw all caution to the wind and committed my gravest sin. I reached out and *touched* him, my hand on his shoulder, fingers splayed wide over hard tendons of muscle before I forced him to turn toward me while he was still on his knees.

Something clattered to the pavement.

A gun.

My blood went ice cold.

So slowly that I was sure he'd take the opportunity to run, I dragged my gaze up the length of his torso. Closer now, I could see all the little details that I'd missed before—the perfectly tailored shirt I'd bought for him was plastered to his skin, emphasizing the width of his shoulders and the muscular planes of his chest. The top buttons were askew, the third one gone, leaving me to imagine him tearing frantically at the material, eager to draw air into his heaving lungs as he hauled his body out of the river.

Because that's what he'd done, hadn't he?

He was soaked. Water droplets still clung to the bare column of his throat, left his full lips shiny and wet, desperate for the press of a lover's kiss. Down at my sides, my fingers curled into tight, aching fists, even as I wrenched my gaze away from my best mate's mouth to finally look him dead in the eye.

"What, couldn't bear to live with the crushing guilt?" I didn't recognize the sound of my voice. It was dark, thick, as if I was the one drowning. Then again, maybe I was. Maybe I'd yet to wake up from the nightmare that was Kirill Volkov taking a leather belt to my fucking back while I twisted and turned in a last-ditch effort to escape the inescapable. I narrowed my eyes on his familiar face, clocking the way he flinched at my question, and then I lowered my voice even more. "Or maybe, Kiryusha . . . you were just waiting for *me*."

"Please," he whispered.

He leaned forward just enough to push the gun toward me, his meaning clear. And while that single flame of fury still danced wild and reckless in my soul, I was mesmerized by the sight of him on his knees, his lashes wet with tears as he blinked up at me in a wordless appeal for me to end him.

He was beautiful.

I'd always thought so, but like this . . . with his emotional shields in ruin around him, it was as if I'd finally been granted access to step into the walled fortress of his heart. And step in, I did. Eagerly. Greedily. Like a man in the desert after finally stumbling upon an oasis, knees hitting hot sand, hands cupping fresh water, throat working with each desperate swallow, drinking more and more until he was damn near sick with it.

That was me.

Sick with want for my best friend.

Sick with *need*.

"Yarik." My name was a plea, rough with regret. "*Please*."

And I picked it up, the gun. Lowered to my haunches right there by the river, with the moonlight exposing all of Kirill's sorrow and all of his shame. I let the weight of the weapon ground me to this moment, to the anger I felt deep inside, the way it flashed hot and cold, all at once, until I was lightheaded from the rush.

I stood.

Lifted my arm.

Pressed the gun to his damp temple, and rasped, "You're a hypocrite, Kirill Volkov. Refusing to let me die and then demanding I put you out of your own bloody misery."

"I know," he rasped back. His cheeks were flushed, his long, elegant fingers biting into the meat of his thighs. He looked like a man in prayer, but instead of bowing his head to God, he kept those somber midnight eyes pinned on me. I searched his features, looking for some hidden motive that I'd somehow missed in all the years I'd known him, but his gaze was wide open and trusting, like now that he'd placed his fate into my hands, he could finally . . . breathe.

I'd stopped breathing in that study.

Even now, I couldn't seem to catch my breath.

"Say it."

"Yarik—"

"I want you to *say* it," I growled. "Tell me why you did it. Tell me why you'd let him—why you'd do that when I asked—when I fucking *begged* y-you. I begged, Kirill." Tears washed to the surface, blurring his moonlit face as I choked back a ragged cry. "I begged, and you didn't stop him. *Y-you* didn't stop. How could you? H-how could you fucking do that to me—"

"Because I'm *selfish!*" he roared. He didn't stand up or push the gun away, but I staggered back, anyway, so startled by the raw emotion bleeding from his expression that I was momentarily struck speechless. "Because I'd drag you down to Hell with me before I ever let you go."

Then he stood.

Unless I was angling for a swim, there was nowhere to escape.

He came for me, fury and regret and something utterly untamed flitting through his gaze just before he snagged me by the wrist, forcing me to put the gun back to his temple. I stared down at him, breathing hard and fast, as he touched his finger to mine, right there where it rested safely beside the trigger.

We'd never been this close.

Never breathed the same air the way we were now, so that if I dared, I could lean down just a little and there'd be no distance between us at all. There'd be him, and there'd be me, and we'd be *together*, in a way we'd never been before.

Yarik and Kirill.

Kirill and Yarik.

I was lost. Lost to the new, unfamiliar sensation of *him* touching *me*. Lost to the heat coursing recklessly through my veins, making the front of my trousers embarrassingly tight as I hardened in my briefs. I was still angry, but worse than that, worse than *anything*, was the fact that I was drowning in hope—*kiss me, kiss me, kiss me.*

"Do it," he demanded in a soft, dangerous murmur. "Kill me, Yarik."

I searched his gaze.

Still breathless.

Still silently begging, *kiss me—kiss me—kiss me—*

"Or what?" I shot back raggedly. "I have to stay with you in Hell?"

His chin tipped up. "Yes."

"Because that's where you belong?"

"I hurt you."

"You did."

"I ruined us."

I licked my lips, then confessed, "We were already ruined, Kiryusha."

"No, we're—"

"Two ruined souls." I pulled the gun back, tugging it out of his grasp, in order to press the carbon-steel mouth to the underside of my chin. "Some days I think we might even be two broken halves of the same whole, where darkness meets shadow. You can't let me go, and I . . . I would rather take my last breath than live even a second without you in it."

"Even in Hell?"

"Yes," I admitted roughly, "even in Hell."

We'd reached a stalemate. He wouldn't kill me, and I wouldn't kill him. Behind me, the rush of the Thames was a stark reminder that we'd spent the last eight years shouldering the gravity of life side by side. Where I fell, he rose, and when he shattered—infrequent as it was—I stayed glued to his side, unwavering in my devotion to him.

We were darkness.

We were shadow.

And there was no denying it, not anymore—I loved Kirill Volkov. Not the way you loved a best mate or a brother. I loved him the way you did a soulmate. With rings and vows and the promise of happily-ever-after. I felt myself straining toward him, aching for a taste. Just one, if that's all I'd ever get. I couldn't—wouldn't—take anything he didn't readily offer me, but that didn't stop my thoughts from racing from one fantasy to the next.

I wanted his lips on mine, his hands gripping my arse, holding me flush against him. I wanted nights where we watched the stars, our fingers tangled between us, and nights when we fucked until we were sweaty and raw and dizzy from the high of coming so hard, we blacked out.

I wanted *everything*.

With him.

The boy I'd found on this riverbank years and years ago, never knowing how that one act of mercy would lead us to this moment, with me holding a gun to the soft, sensitive place beneath my chin, one trigger-pull away from ending it all.

I want you, I almost whispered.

Please tell me you want me, too.

Before I could scrounge up the nerve, he muttered,

"I'll never forgive myself," and it was that quick, how fast reality crashed back down on me. Because as Kirill made me hand over the gun, and I watched him tuck it into his waistband, it became glaringly obvious that while I'd been hoping we might lead to more, he was hoping that we would never end.

"You're my best mate," he said to me quietly, standing so close that I could feel his warm breath on my skin. But where anticipation had wound tight across my muscles before, now I was achingly aware of hope—stupid, fucking hope—withering to ash within me. "My only family," he added, briefly meeting my gaze before he looked away as if this confession, more than any other, was too much for him. "I'll spend the rest of my life earning your trust back, Yarik, I swear. I'm sorry. I'm so . . . I'm just so fucking *sorry*."

My heart was cold.

My back was aching.

I was sorry, too. Sorry that for one breathless second, I thought that I could really have it all. Him and me together, with rings and vows and the promise of happily-ever-after. Forever.

There was no greater fool alive than me.

CHAPTER SEVENTEEN

Deleted Yarik Text:
You're a fucking wanker, you know that?

I mean, Russia??? You HATE Russia.

You left me.

You left and I

I don't know what to say to you. Or rather, I know all the things I want to say but we don't say those things. Not to each other. Which means I don't say them to anyone at all because I'm apparently fucked in the head enough to think that maybe, one day, you might look at me and realize that you

YARIK

Heard Father sent you to your favorite city on Earth. Any idea when you're coming home?

YARIK

Hey

Deleted Yarik Text:
You've been gone twenty-three days and I think...

I think this is the longest we've ever gone without talking.

Even when you fake-hated me, you never ignored me, and I'm trying really hard not to go mad with worry. If something bad happened to you, I'm sure I would have heard the news by now. But I . . .

I miss you

I miss you so much. Please come back

Deleted Yarik Text:
I haven't slept in days

Every time I close my eyes, I remember what happened in the study. I remember looking at you, thinking you were my hero. Then I blinked and you became someone else

The monster I never thought to look for under my bed.

The villain whose heart is stained black but there are cracks, fissures, which offer glimpses of light. I can still feel the way you pushed me against the wall, how my hands turned clammy and all I heard was the sound of my own heartbeat hammering in my ears. I waited for you to save me, the way you always have but

I understand

I wish that I didn't.

That's really what keeps me up at night—that I understand. How could I not?

You left, and I have no idea when you'll be back, or if you're even still alive, and every day I think to myself . . .

I would chain you to me, if I could

I would be the monster under your bed. The villain who bides his time, waiting for when you least expect it to strike

If I had my way, Kiryusha, I would never let you go

But I think . . . I think you've already gone. And I don't know how to get you back.

Deleted Yarik Text:
If you've died, at least have the common decency to fucking haunt me, you prick

YARIK

Tomorrow I'm being made into a brigadier

If you're not dead, I'm gonna need you to come and put a bullet in my brain

Also, go fuck yourself.

CHAPTER EIGHTEEN

YARIK

In the Bratva, it was common for a brigadier to pick his own foot soldiers—men you trusted to have your back when shit went sideways and all you had were your wits to save you.

My father either hadn't gotten the memo, or he'd decided that the best way to deal with an unruly heir was to publicly humiliate him so thoroughly that he never questioned his place within the syndicate's social hierarchy again.

I questioned everything.

Daily.

With my back pressed against the wall of my father's study, I breathed in slowly through my nose, never taking my eyes off my sperm donor. He sat at his oversized desk like a tyrant: loafers planted on the floor; thick, ring-clad fingers clasped over a still-flat stomach; the expensive watch on his wrist glinting under the overhead light. Petr Volkov exuded power every second of the day. If he'd ever approached the world differently, I couldn't remember it. And even if he had, what did it matter? All he wanted was to strip away what was left of my pride until there was nothing left.

He wanted me begging.

Wanted me throwing a bloody fit, like a toddler with a tantrum.

Wasn't going to happen, not even if the red-headed bloke occupying the chair across from him kept darting wary looks in my direction. Looks that said he was fully aware that nothing about this meeting was remotely normal, and he wasn't about to become fodder in a war that didn't involve him.

Couldn't blame him, really. I was tired of fighting this battle, too.

Too bad Father wasn't willing to put down his sword.

"My son is reckless," he clipped out. "Impulsive. He was expelled from every boarding school in the country, and against all hope to the contrary, age hasn't managed to do him any favors. He is worse now."

Worse. Right. Because I'd had the gall to refuse signing anything that would have bound me to Giulia Accardi for the rest of my miserable fucking life.

I bit the inside of my cheek so hard, the delicate skin broke. As the metallic taste of blood flooded my mouth, I knotted my trembling hands into even tighter fists at the base of my spine. Notched my chin high, too, doing my best to look unbothered.

Try harder.

Don't let him see. Don't let anyone *see that you're—*

It wasn't getting any easier. I'd thought it might. Call me delusional, an emotional wreck, a disappointment, whatever, but every time I crossed the threshold of Father's study, I found myself hoping that these visits, which had increased in frequency over the last six months, might soften the edges of the memories that continued to stalk my dreams. Exposure therapy, I heard it called.

Yeah. Well.

One visit, two visits, a hundred. Didn't fucking matter. My reaction to these four walls was as visceral today as it had been that night when I'd stood with my wrists bound above my head while the boy I loved whipped my back raw.

Now he's gone.

He's been *gone.*

And you know he isn't coming back.

Something hot and sickly twisted in my gut. Desolation probably. My new constant companion. Another abscess that would never heal because every time I picked at the scab, all I did was reopen the wound and feel ten times worse afterward.

I wasn't sleeping. I barely managed to eat.

It was probably a good thing no one but my little sister paid me any bit of attention, and even then, we weren't all that close. Had never been, really. It was easy to blame my years' long stint in Moscow, but the reality was, Father had kept us separated from childhood, putting us on two separate paths that never collided. By the time I'd come back from Russia, neither of us had put much energy into building a bond. Nina had her own shit to worry about, never mind taking on the burden of mine.

The war we waged made us solitary creatures.

Which was why Father cherry-picking the men in my unit made me want to scream. It was just another point of leverage to hold over my head. Instead of being loyal to me, my soldiers would be spies for him. Would they report back everything I did, everything I *said?* The thought of having no privacy at all made my hands shake even more.

I was already living under a microscope.

My new bodyguard, Anton, kept tabs on me. Uncle Igor kept tabs on me. My father's brigadiers kept tabs on me. I couldn't even piss without someone standing outside the stall. What did they think I'd do? Fucking off myself right over the toilet? Things had been strained before, but these days they were downright unbearable. I was *suffocating*.

And now my only hope of carving out a slice of purgatory for myself—because no way a place like Heaven could be real, not with what I saw every day—was slim to bloody none.

"I've been advised to keep him out of business matters, but . . ." Father drummed a silent beat with his thumbs against his abdomen. He spoke carefully as if picking his way through a landmine that he himself hadn't staged. "It is my personal opinion that to make such a move would prove detrimental in the long run. It will invite questions. Gossip. No, better to put him in the hands of a trusted few who have the experience to keep him on the straight and narrow, wouldn't you say, Beck?"

Like many of the soldiers within the Volkov organization, including Kirill, Beck wasn't Russian. And just like Kirill, Beck had learned to speak the language fluently. It was my father's preferred form of indoctrination—finding people from all walks of life and then treating them to the same insular form of "brotherhood" that had worked for La Cosa Nostra or the Yakuza, who didn't allow outsiders within their ranks.

Russian in soul, if not in blood. That was Petr Volkov's motto.

So it wasn't much of a surprise that Daniel Beck, a freckled Behemoth who'd grown up on a council estate right outside London, replied to my father in perfect Russian: "What if I say no?"

That caught my attention.

I stared at Beck so hard, I was sure he could feel it, but he didn't acknowledge me in any way. Instead, he reclined in his chair with the sort of cocky, self-assured confidence that straightened my spine. Was he—there was no way he'd actually—

"Thing is, Mr. Volkov, I'm not lookin' to be a glorified nanny."

Holy. Fuck. Daniel Beck had a death wish.

Into the icy stillness that followed, Father bit off, "Excuse me?"

"A nanny." Beck rested one ankle on his opposite knee, then settled his hands over his upraised shin. "Someone to wipe your son's arse, Mr. Volkov. That's what you're really after, innit? Want me watching your son's every move—when he shits, when he fucks, when he's not being a very good boy. Let me know if I've got it wrong."

Bloody hell, he was absolutely mad.

Certifiably *mental*.

My gaze pinged back to my father, who looked completely flustered. A vein throbbed in his temple. My stomach flipped. Had he ever been talked to like that? I didn't think so. Then again, if someone had, they were probably long gone by now. Luckily, while Beck might have a death wish, he wouldn't end up dead just yet. Too many people knew about this meeting. Just this morning, I'd watched one of Beck's mates grab him by the shoulder for a friendly, excited shake. No doubt his friends thought he was getting promoted.

To something *besides* babysitting the boss's eighteen-year-old son.

Daniel Beck settled deeper into his seat. Over his flat belly, he tangled his fingers together, such a picture-perfect mirror of my father that something terribly giddy flooded my veins.

"I should kill you." Father's voice wavered with fury.

"You won't."

"The *mouth* on you."

Beck smiled. That was it. He just—*smiled*. Like this was all some big laugh.

I'd never seen my father more agitated in my entire life.

His fists came down like gavels on the desk. "You will apologize."

"Will I?"

"Yes," Father bit out from behind gritted teeth. "You will."

"Nah. Don't think I will."

My father's mouth opened incredulously. And then it snapped shut.

Beck took the opportunity to add, "I'm your last option, ain't I?" He flicked a dismissive glance in my direction, one that might have had me shifting with embarrassment thirty minutes ago but one that I chose to ignore now because there was *magic* happening in this room, and I didn't even care that it was at my expense. I watched Beck's lips part in another little smile. "In case you 'aven't noticed, no one is knocking down your door to be wiping your son's arse, Mr. Volkov."

Adrenaline swept over my body in a flash of heat,

lighting that reckless fire within me that had been battered down to almost nothing in the last six months. It danced and spluttered, begging to be set aflame, and I opened my mouth to feed it oxygen. To let it burn everything within reach, if only to catch a glimmer of my former self.

"How much do you want?"

At the sound of my voice, Beck's head snapped my way. "What?"

The surprise on his face said that I'd caught him off guard. I didn't bother to look at my father. Nor did I bother with stepping forward. I kept my back to the wall, my trembling hands protected at the base of my spine, and repeated, "How much do you want?"

Auburn brows drew together in bewilderment. The slope of his nose was slightly off-center, but I didn't see a scar or the tell-tale ridge that might indicate the fragile cartilage breaking at some point in the past. His nose was simply crooked. The only imperfection in an otherwise perfectly symmetrical face. I wondered if, in another life, he might have found himself on a runway in Milan or New York or Paris. If he'd spent so long clawing himself out of poverty that I could look at a face as classically handsome as his and only see glimpses of Hell in his hazel-green eyes.

Like the Devil, Daniel Beck caught on quick.

Those hazel eyes flared with delight. "You'll be a pain in my arse, I'm sure."

No point in pretending otherwise. "Yes. I will be."

"I'll want to kill you."

"Probably."

"Maybe you'll want to kill me."

The smile I leveled on him was akin to a snake ready to strike. "Never."

He laughed.

The fucking bastard threw back his head and *laughed*, and swear to bloody God, Father looked ready to implode. It didn't deter him. Beck, I mean. He only held my gaze for a beat longer than was socially acceptable, like he was seeing me as more than some pampered, self-absorbed prince, then rose to his feet. The shift in position had him staring down his crooked nose at my father, a fact that he seemed to relish as he announced, "I'll let your son decide my wage."

It was an olive branch. An offer of good faith that I wouldn't fuck him over.

More than that, it was Daniel Beck handing me power on a silver platter. Eighteen years of drawing air into my lungs and I'd never stood a chance of winning even the smallest battles against Petr Volkov. I bled and I bled, and I kept on bleeding until it became something of a miracle that my body continued to fight at all, even when I was gasping and bruised and broken. Just shards of glass littered across a dirty floor. You could piece me back together and still, the reflection that stared back would never be whole.

So maybe I was broken, but for the first time that I could remember, I smiled. For real. The muscles around my mouth ached from disuse. Beck must have recognized something familiar in the awkward gesture because he smiled back. This one, more than any of his others, was real, too. And just as rusty as mine.

Without a word to my father, he moved away from the desk and strode toward me. When he stood a foot away, he bowed his head a little. Russet strands fell across his temple but not before I saw a wicked grin flit across his lips.

"Happy to be of service, my liege."

Cocky bastard.

My lips twitched.

Then he was gone, leaving Father and I to rot away in the terrible silence that followed. I kept my gaze on the empty doorway. Kept my hands hidden, too, because if he saw any weakness at all, I'd be fucked. There was a creak of wood and then muffled footsteps. They approached. One step, two. Another and another, and then my sperm donor was standing way too close, his breath hot on my chin.

Because I was taller now.

Give me a few years and maybe I'd double his weight, too.

Something about that—knowing my days of appearing young and naïve were numbered—made me smile. This one was just as real as the one I'd given Beck, but it was also reckless and impulsive and wholly *me*.

I turned my head just enough to meet eyes the same color blue as my own. "Daniel Beck is perfect, I think. Exactly the sort of soldier I want by my side." My slow, dark smile ticked wider. "Let me know if you find another just like him, yeah?"

I walked away before my father could get out a word.

Power tasted *divine*.

CHAPTER NINETEEN

YARIK

You'll be happy to know that I've two soldiers under me now. Daniel Beck is the first—I think you know him, or at least know of him? Mid-twenties. Red hair. He's a God, Kiryusha.

No, don't laugh. Because I know you are.

Bloke is downright mental. Looked Father right in the eye and practically told him to fuck off. So, yeah. That makes him a God in my book—albeit a God who doesn't give a rat's arse about pleasantries, and if I ever catch him on his knees, it won't be on account of him praying.

Anyway.

Eren Doğan is the other. He's quieter than Beck but not as quiet as you. He's intense like you, too. Focused.

Deleted Yarik Text:
When are you coming home

YARIK

> His Russian isn't that great. English is his second language, after Turkish. I won't deny that I was being selfish when I picked him. I like the idea of being surrounded by people who don't fit Father's little vision of what it means to be attached to the Volkov name.

Deleted Yarik Text:

I wish that I wasn't a Volkov

I wish that I could run away to wherever you are

YARIK

> Do you ever think of me?

> Fuck

> wrong text

Deleted Yarik Text:

I didn't mean

stupid bloody fucking vodka

I hate vodka

I also hate Russia or Moscow or wherever it is that you've been sent to

are you in Yakutsk?

is that what happened, Kiryusha? Are you frozen to death, maybe? So numb that you can't pick up your bloody phone and send me a text that says

I AM ALIVE

see? three words? not that hard. then I'd know you are, in fact, breathing

are you still breathing?

> YARIK
>
> Sorry about last night. Had one too many with Beck.
>
> Eren gave me judgmental looks from across the table, though, so it was almost like you were there.
>
> Also, vodka is the devil. I'm never drinking it again.

Deleted Yarik Text:
I went down to our spot by the river last night.

I'm not sure when I started thinking of it as that—our spot. Laughable, really. Like it's not where I almost killed you and you almost killed me but

It was raining, you know. The sky felt positively wounded. Battering cries and trembling earth and black, menacing clouds that split in two only long enough to let through a blade of light. I ended up under the big oak tree, the one with the branches that hang so low, you can walk right on up. The tree you once said belonged in *Lord of the Rings*.

I couldn't see worth a damn.

I was soaked to the bone, shivering my arse off, thinking bloody stupid stuff. Fanciful, really. Things like, maybe you've been taken. Maybe I've been sitting here for months, angry that you're gone, when you've been made a prisoner. I imagined you locked behind bars, desperate and hurting and hungry, and that

That broke something inside me, Kiryusha.

How I could be so self-centered to think, for even a second, that you wouldn't come back to England if you were given the option. Of course there's no option. Of course something's gone wrong.

I sat there in the rain, huddled under the tree, sobbing from the thoughts racing through my head. That you might never find your way home. That, wherever you are, you must be left to darkness with no stars to guide you back to me like Ptolemy and his queen

then the sun came out this morning, like the storm never happened at all, and I overheard Artem tell my father that you'd been at a party in Moscow last night, socializing with oligarchs, with some pretty girl on your arm, and I

I want to hate you

I just want to HATE you

And I do, Kiryusha. I hate you for leaving. I hate you for making me think, for even one second, that I might matter to you as much as you matter to me. I hate you for every minute of the last eight months of silence but I—

I hate that I love you so much, I write you these stupid fucking texts just to pretend that maybe you might write back one day and tell me that you love me too

CHAPTER TWENTY

YARIK

As luck would have it, I was handling business when Kirill made his grand return.

And by "handling business," I meant that I was trying to persuade a reluctant buyer from America when the door clicked open, and in walked my father with Kirill at his side.

I froze.

There really was no other way to describe the mortifying way my bones stiffened in surprise or how every intelligent thought fell right out of my head before disappearing into thin air like smoke.

What was he doing here?

And why was he hiding in my father's shadow?

Like a lovesick knob, I thrust all questions aside to soak in my best friend's familiar gait striding deeper into the room. I almost jumped to my feet. Fuck, did I want to —anything to close the distance between us faster—but the stiff, almost aloof expression on Kirill's face held me back. Patience. *Breathe.* Not wanting to come across like an overeager puppy, I dug my fingers into the wooden armrests of the fifteenth-century chair I sat on, determined to maintain some modicum of self-control.

Outwardly, at least.

On the inside, I was a right bloody mess.

Any second now, he was going to look my way. He probably wouldn't smile because his smiles were rare, precious things, but his gaze would warm, and that . . . that would be enough, just to know that he was as excited to see me as I was to see him.

Nine months.

He'd been gone *nine months*.

Anticipation kicked my pulse into a full-fledged sprint. Against the backdrop of pale green wallpaper, Kirill looked as if he'd just come from a funeral. Black suit. Black shirt. Black shoes. His midnight-black eyes skimmed right past me to land on Robert Murray, seemingly clocking the Irish mobster's reluctance in just one glance.

I felt the brush-off like a hot brand on my skin.

Heat rose to my cheeks—a flush that I couldn't hide, not with my complexion. And still, I didn't look away because, apparently, I was a glutton for punishment.

Kiryusha, please. Just—

It was like I didn't even exist.

Instead, he studied Murray as he would a bug trapped under a jar while I tried, and failed, to wrench my gaze away before I got caught staring. The last nine months had left their mark on him. His hair was shorter than I remembered it being, the silky strands slicked back to reveal sharp cheekbones and an even sharper jawline. He was paler, too, his normally warm olive skin appearing almost sallow in the late afternoon light, like he'd been abandoned somewhere without sun.

Russia could do that to a person.

Take all that warmth and turn it into ice.

And it was ice that I felt creeping into my bones the longer I waited for Kirill to acknowledge my presence. Seconds bled into seconds. My heartbeat thundered in my ears while my palms turned clammy. Surreptitiously, I ran them along the length of my thighs and hoped no one noticed. Then, just when I thought Kirill might finally glance my way, he turned from the Irishman to stare straight ahead, unblinking, like all the brainless twats Father insisted on hiring as his personal bodyguards.

My jaw almost fell open.

What happened to you? hovered on the tip of my tongue. *Blink twice if you've been drugged.*

Something brushed my elbow.

Too focused on Kirill, I lurched to the left, startled, only to realize too late that it was my father drawing to a stop beside me. "Please, carry on," he said almost pleas-antly—right before he dropped a hand onto my shoulder and squeezed, hard. "Don't stop on our account."

He stood too close. I could smell the cloying scent of his cologne. I could—I could *feel* his expectation even as threads of nervous energy had me flexing my fingers where they rested on my thighs. Why not take one of the empty seats? There were plenty of them scattered all over the room. Better yet, why hadn't Beck or Eren let me know that the doors to this meeting were about to be blown wide open, and the one man we universally hated ushered inside? Never mind the fact that Kirill was *here*, in London, and he hadn't said a word to me about it.

Kirill, who still wouldn't look at me.

The situation was so fucked, I didn't know whether to laugh or cry.

As it was, it took every bit of self-awareness I possessed to wipe the lingering shock from Father's arrival off my face. Only then did I turn my attention back to Robert Murray. Galway-born but currently based out of Chicago, he'd crossed the Atlantic just to have this conversation with me in person. I couldn't risk cocking it all up now, especially not with Father literally breathing down my neck.

Inhaling slowly, I pressed my fingertips into my thighs for three solid seconds and then exhaled, letting it all go—the anxiety that had sat heavy in my gut all morning, the emotional rush over seeing Kirill for the first time in months. I couldn't waste time dwelling on any of it, not when I only had one chance to get this right.

Snagging the decanter of Irish whiskey off the table, I made a show of pouring two fingers worth into a crystal tumbler. The shift in position shook off my father's hold, and I released another tight breath from the clutch of my lungs. When I finally pushed the drink in Murray's direction, his lips curled upward with appreciation.

"The Emerald Isle, eh?" With a chuff of glee, he shook his head as if he couldn't even believe the value of the amber-gold currently cradled in the palm of his hand. "Heard the last one of these sold at an auction in Nashville for two-point-eight-mill."

"It did."

"To you?"

"No."

Murray blinked in surprise. "You're telling me all that noise about it being the last of its kind was a scam?"

"Not a scam." Carefully, I set the triple-distilled, single-malt whiskey aside. The glass clinked against the marble tabletop. "Scarcity sells. It's just business."

He looked from me to the decanter and then back to me again. A streak of boldness flickered in his dark brown eyes. "How many bottles do you have?"

I only smiled.

"That many, yeah?" Another shake of his head, this time accompanied by a playful chuckle. It didn't sit right. That good attitude of his felt slippery at best, dodgy at worst. Even though I hated the idea of doing business with someone I didn't trust, I'd learned over the years that in the shadowy depths of the criminal underworld, everyone hid behind a mask. Murray's just happened to piss me off more than most. "So," he said, "where were we?"

"You were telling me why you weren't interested in our product."

With a flinch he couldn't quite cover up, he darted a quick glance at Kirill.

I had to close my hands into fists under the table to keep from doing the same.

"Ah. Right." He sipped his whiskey, clearly buying time before having to provide an answer in front of one of the most dangerous arms dealers in the world. The same man who owned, funded, and profited billions off the product Robert Murray was now tiptoeing around. He hadn't been this indecisive when we'd talked on the phone last week. "Thing is, you see"—he offered a strained laugh—"my boss isn't sure how he feels about . . ."

"About what?"

"About what it is that you're selling."

Beside me, Father shifted his weight.

I didn't have to look at him to sense his mounting displeasure. It rippled across the room in an all-consuming wave that made me want to curl into a ball, if only to withstand the storm.

Pathetic.

Shame crawled up my throat as I tamped down every instinct that told me to run. The truth was that I was almost nineteen years old, and Petr Volkov still scared me. I could hide that fear behind reckless, devil-may-care behavior, and I could bury it, deep, when the situation called for it, but facts were facts: my father's moods were volatile, and I bore the scars as living proof.

Desperate as I was to run, I couldn't, not from Robert Murray.

This was my chance to prove that I wasn't stupid, no matter what Father or his peers thought of me. I'd been the one to see an opportunity present itself after hearing rumors that Murray's boss, Connor O'Brien, was thinking about breaking ties with his current distributor. Considering O'Brien's stronghold on all of Chicago, despite frequent attempts from the Italians to dislodge him from his throne, I figured there was room to maneuver us into a mutually beneficial partnership. I also knew my father was keen to start operations in the States as early as next year—even though I only had that information because I'd overheard him discussing possible timelines with Artem, who still operated as his councilor. Either way, I couldn't let this chance slip right through my fingers. Too much was resting on my shoulders.

After a steadying breath, I shored up my resolve and pulled on a mask of my own.

The one of the ruthless mafia prince.

"Spell it out for me," I murmured. "What exactly does Mr. O'Brien have a problem with?"

Murray's lips twitched uneasily. "You traffic ghost guns."

Fuck, my father hated that term.

I didn't dare look over at him.

Beneath the table, my nails bit into my palms hard enough to draw blood. "I'm not sure that I see the issue. They aren't serialized, but some might argue that's better for everyone involved. Less chance of authorities realizing you've gotten your hands dirty if things go tits up."

"It's not that I . . ." He cleared his throat. "My *boss* feels like this isn't how it's done."

"How *what* isn't done?"

"Business."

"Because?"

Stiffly, he replied, "There's no honor in it."

"But there's honor in spilling the blood of innocents? The wives of your enemies? Their children? What's your definition of honor, Mr. Murray? I'm curious."

It was, I realized a second too late, the complete wrong approach.

Robert Murray's features twisted with so much dislike, not even a three-million-dollar bottle of whiskey could bring this deal back from the dead. It was one thing to push for a business arrangement and another thing entirely to offend someone's sense of morality. Even the worst of humanity had their own code of conduct, and I'd just bludgeoned Murray's to pieces.

Fuck.

Fuck.

Fuck—

"Would you like my personal opinion, Mr. Murray?" Father's hand returned to my shoulder, which he yanked on so hard, I let out a low grunt as my spine collided with the chair's tall backrest. Then he dug in his nails, like claws, pinning me in place. "I find it curious that you've come here alone."

Wary brown eyes darted right then left, probably taking note of the men who stood like silent sentinels around the perimeter of the room. Anton, I knew, never let me out of his sight. Murray rolled one shoulder in a too-casual shrug. "I don't travel with bodyguards."

"No travel companions?" Father asked.

"Don't feel necessary. It's a quick trip."

"Kirill, if you will. Please."

Unable to move, all I could do was watch my best friend step forward. In his hand was a shiny new mobile, the exact make and model that I had tucked into the front pocket of my trousers. He'd cut his hair, grown pale from the lack of sun, ignored me as if I didn't even exist, but this . . . this felt like the cruelest change of all. Maybe it was stupid to think that the phone I'd given him would last forever, but he'd always seemed to treasure it, choosing to forego upgrades just to keep his old, imperfect one.

Did it finally break?

Or had he tossed it away, as ready to be done with it as he seemed to be with me?

Without even realizing it, I'd leaned forward as if I could knock the device out of his hand, but Father tightened his grip, jerking me back into place like I was nothing but a wayward child.

My nostrils flared.

Fuck him and fuck this—

Kirill planted one hand on the back of the Irishman's chair and set the phone down on the table in front of him with the other. He didn't pull away, just caged Robert

Murray in, so that the man's only chance at escape was to his right. Then again, that wouldn't get him anywhere, either, not with Anton and the other guards holding their positions.

I went perfectly still.

Something . . . something wasn't right.

Bending forward until they were cheek to cheek, Kirill turned his head just enough that his lips nearly grazed the man's ear. When he spoke, his voice was a low, dark rumble, barely loud enough to be heard over the surge of adrenaline whistling in my ears: "Press play."

All color leeched from Murray's face.

"I don't—I don't think that's necessary," he stuttered awkwardly, but Kirill wasn't having it. The hand that he'd left on the chair clamped down on the man's nape, forcing his head at a severely sharp angle so the only thing in Murray's vision had to be the phone laid out on the table before him.

"Go on, then," my best friend murmured. "We're waiting."

For a second, nothing happened.

And then with visibly shaking fingers, Robert Murray did as he was told. There wasn't any sound, so I couldn't tell what exactly played out on the phone, but I watched his features carefully, tracking each emotion as they rolled swiftly from one to the next. Dread. Terror. Regret. Murray flattened one hand on the table as if it was the only thing keeping him upright.

Kirill kept his voice low, conversational. "Who are they?"

"I don't know."

"Are you sure?"

Murray's throat clicked with an audible swallow. "Yes."

"Let's see if this refreshes your memory." Without removing his hand from the Irishman's nape, Kirill used his other to swipe to the next picture or video. He didn't wait for Murray, just tapped the screen and let the evidence speak for itself.

There was sound this time.

Two male voices echoed down the length of a hallway. While their words were muddled, thanks to them speaking over each other, I could hear the distinct squeal of rubber soles against tiled floor like they were in a rush, maybe even sprinting down the hall. Before the video could play any longer, Kirill said, "Pause it."

With misery etched into the drawn lines of his face, Murray obeyed.

"Cormac Kelly. Sean Lynch." Kirill paused for a heartbeat. "Still don't know them?"

"No," Murray whispered.

Kirill hummed noncommittedly, and then he hit play.

Hell was watching your loved one murdered right there in front of you, but Hell was also watching a loved one turn into a stranger before your very eyes. As Cormac Kelly and Sean Lynch begged for their lives, I watched my best friend become someone utterly unrecognizable.

"I commend you for the effort," he said over the screams of dying men, "really, I do. Spreading rumors that your boss was on the outs with your distributor? Offering to come all the way to London, only to change your mind once you got here? Solid plan. Quality acting. You almost had it, Mr. Murray. Problem is, we have eyes all over the UK."

Robert closed his own eyes in defeat.

"We knew the minute you all touched down in Heathrow," Kirill uttered softly. "We knew when you went your separate ways, when you stayed in the accommodations Yaroslav here was kind enough to book for you, and even when Mr. Kelly and Mr. Lynch went and found their own place. We knew the minute you told Mr. O'Brien that your accomplices had found a way into our warehouse, and we knew, although they didn't, that it was a trap."

Thick, wretched tension consumed the room.

Murray braced his hands against the edge of the table, his pupils nothing more than tiny, black pinpricks in a pool of anxious brown.

"Phone your boss," Kirill said.

"I don't—"

"Your boss, Mr. Murray. Go on."

At some point, I'd curled my hands over the armrests of my chair. Father kept his hold on me, but I wasn't trying to run away. I was stunned into compliance. Heart thrashing wildly, pulse beating to a rhythm that whispered only one thing: *What have you done?* And then louder, more frantic: *Whathaveyoudonewhathaveyoudonewhathaveyoudone?*

I didn't know.

Fuck, I didn't know, and now—

"Murray," a thickly accented voice came over the line, the man's relief starkly evident in the heavy breath that shuddered across the expanse of an ocean. "Thank Christ. Have you heard from Cormac? Sean? This hairbrained idea of yours better not have gotten the lot of you into any troub—"

"Hello, Mr. O'Brien."

If I'd been stunned into compliance before, then

Connor O'Brien was currently too stunned to speak. It took him five solid seconds to splutter back an answer: "I . . . Hello, yes. That is, am I speaking with Petr Volkov?"

Father didn't bother with niceties. "Did you think to take advantage of my son?"

Like Murray, I felt all the blood drain from my face.

"What?" The line crackled with the sound of uncomfortable laughter. "No, of course not."

"You are not a very good liar." O'Brien's laughter stilled, but before he could say anything, my father continued in his clipped, central Russian accent, "Let me present to you my dilemma—you sent your men to London to sneak into my warehouses, to either take what does not belong to them or, worse, you planned to bring home knowledge that would see me out of business while you stole everything that I have spent thirty years building. Which is it?"

O'Brien said nothing.

"Ah, the liar does not speak." Dark amusement glittered in my father's tone. "Do you—what do the Americans say? Do you stay silent so that you do not need to plead the fifth?"

"I don't need to plead the fifth for anything. We've done nothing wrong."

"The security footage I have says otherwise."

"*Your* security footage, I presume?" O'Brien's voice sharpened. "I'm supposed to just believe whatever you say, yeah? I don't think so."

"Perhaps not. Perhaps I shall let your Robert Murray do the talking while he still can."

"Keep your bloody fuckin' hands off him," O'Brien growled, "or you'll regret it."

"What will I regret?" The hand on my shoulder flexed. "You have tiny Chicago while I have the world."

"Connor," Murray piped up, beseechingly, while he grasped the whiskey I'd poured him the way a dead man clings to the last vestiges of life. Anything else he might have said died on the tip of his tongue when Kirill—*my* Kirill—pressed a handgun to the back of the man's skull.

Fuck.

Wait.

"Drink up," Kirill said, and then he—oh, fucking hell—

Warmth splattered my chin, my neck, the corner of my mouth. The incredibly rare bottle of Emerald's Isle tipped over from the force of the blast, the glass painted with brain matter while the trunk of Robert Murray's body seemed to hover in place, listing slightly forward, before he went chest-down on the table with a heavy *thud*, his skull half-gone.

My stomach heaved.

If anything else was said to Connor O'Brien, I didn't hear it, not over the rush of blood roaring in my ears. In the minutes that followed, life carried on in a series of snapshots. I blinked, and Father had stepped away. I blinked again, and there was Kirill, already taking care of cleanup, like this was all part of some grand master plan that I hadn't received an invitation for. I blinked once more, and Anton was grabbing me by the elbow and dragging me out of the antique chair that had once cushioned some medieval king's arse.

I turned to look at it, expecting to see damage, only to find that it'd been spared.

Glancing down, I found the same couldn't be said

about myself. I was covered in blood, remains, and fuck knows what else.

If I could have stripped out of my skin, I would have done so in a heartbeat.

"Yaroslav."

At the sound of my father's voice, I forced myself to lift my chin and search him out with my gaze. He stood by the door, somehow managing to look completely pristine while I might as well have tromped through each of Dante's Nine Circles of Hell. Caked in fresh blood, I waited, heart pounding furiously, while he slowly took me in. Only when he finished did he bother to speak: "You are an embarrassment to this family. Be grateful I don't put you down like a dog."

Then he gestured for Kirill to follow him out the door.

Neither of them stopped to look back at me.

CHAPTER TWENTY-ONE

YARIK

I was, as they say, three sheets to the fucking wind when someone knocked on my bedroom door later that night.

From my spot on the floor, I glared at whoever thought it was a good time to come round mine for what, a little company? Some titillating conversation? Not bloody likely. I wasn't in the mood.

You are an embarrassment—

As I tipped the liquor bottle up to my mouth for another swig, I was sorely tempted to drain the damn thing dry. Lucky for me, I didn't have any plans for the rest of the evening other than to get absolutely pissed off my arse. Way I saw it, if I wasn't hammered by midnight, then it was my personal responsibility to crack open another bottle and take that smarmy cunt, Fate, into my own two hands. Who was around to stop me? Literally nobody.

The doorknob jiggled.

"Open up, Volkov." *Eren.*

"Go away," I mumbled into the bottle, barely staying

upright. "I'm not in the mood for your sanci—santo—*sanctimonious* face right now."

"I'll pick the lock."

"You don't know how to pick a lock."

"Then I'll get Beck to do it for me."

I groaned. "Please don't. I'm fine."

"You're not fine." I had the sudden, blurry visual of Eren pressing a hand to the door. Knowing him, he was probably calculating how much trouble he'd get in for busting the damn thing down. "I'm worried about you, *kardeş*. We both are."

Letting my head fall back against the mattress, I squeezed my eyes shut.

The overprotective prick was right. I wasn't fine.

I'd had my arse handed to me today. Humiliated on such a public stage that I could still hear my father's bodyguards whispering behind my back after I'd stumbled away from Robert Murray's dead body. Their whispers were a poison with no antidote. I'd barely made it back to my room before dropping to my knees, hands cradling my throbbing head, wishing that I could wipe the last twenty-four hours from memory. Booze probably wasn't the healthy solution, but oblivion was preferable to knowing that I was officially the laughingstock of the Bratva.

At any time, someone could have given me the heads-up that Murray was just a vessel for Connor O'Brien to get his hands on some of the "ghost guns" he claimed to hate so much. They could have brought me into the fold. Let me work with them instead of being left to stand on my own. My own father hadn't bothered.

Kirill hadn't either.

I felt my throat close up, and—*fuck me.* With a gasp, I

dropped the bottle against my thigh and pressed the heels of my palms to my closed eyelids. Tears burned to the surface. Each sharp breath rattled my lungs. Stupid. Stupid. Stupid—

"Volkov." The doorknob shook. "Volkov, open the damn door."

I couldn't.

There was no way I could let him see me like this.

Clutching the alcohol in one hand, I turned until I was flush against the mattress but curled onto my side, right arm slung around my bent knees. "Tomorrow," I rasped into the shell of my body. "Come back tomorrow."

With a curse, Eren slammed what I could only assume was his fist against the door before he growled, "I'm getting Beck."

The eerie quiet that came with his absence haunted me.

Years ago, Vera had called me soft. I hadn't understood what she meant, and if I was being honest, at least with myself, I still didn't understand, not really. But it had to be this—this awful feeling of *incompetence* that followed every stage of my life. I wasn't like Kirill or Beck or even my father—men who all seemed to read between the lines to everything that wasn't said out loud.

There were lines, and I read them.

I didn't think it was an intelligence thing; I knew that I was smart. Besides the obvious expulsions, I did all right in school. I scored decent marks, could follow any one of my father's lengthy tangents, and had even helped Volkov Enterprise in the design of a new long-range rifle that the British military had paid good money to get their hands on.

I could kill a man with my eyes closed. Hell, I could do

it with my hands tied behind my back or even in the middle of a storm with heavy winds blowing off the cliffs of Dover. Not a metaphor. I'd done it all, and I hadn't struggled one bit.

So why did everyone dance around me?

Why was I always stuck on the outside when I was destined to inherit the entire Volkov empire? And what other situations had I read wrong?

A knock sounded on the door.

I didn't have it in me to yell at Eren and Beck to go away, not when they only wanted to help. Our little tripod was still finding its footing, which meant that I was acutely aware of the fact that everything I did, everything I said, impacted the way we functioned as a unit. While I hated the idea of them thinking less of me for not opening the door, if they saw the tear tracks on my cheeks . . . Well, I wasn't sure how we'd come back from that. This was the Bratva, wasn't it? And in the Bratva, men didn't cry.

The lump in my throat told me that I didn't deserve a kingdom. I didn't deserve anything at all.

A second later, someone knocked again, harder this time.

Curling into myself even tighter, I let my head drop down onto my bent knees. They'd go away. All I had to do was wait them out and—

The door cracked open.

My head flew up just as a figure stepped into my room. I'd expected Beck or Eren, or even the two of them together in an obvious attempt to ambush me, and my heart stopped beating altogether when the haze of alcohol lifted to reveal the face that haunted my dreams.

Honestly, the goddamn audacity.

I was off the floor a moment later, flying at him with raised fists. "Get out," I snarled, half out of my mind with fury and hurt and betrayal. "Get the *fuck* out of here before I—"

In one swift, unexpected move, Kirill had me laid out on my back. Dazed, I blinked up at the ceiling and gasped for air, fumbling a hand toward my throat where I could still feel the warm clutch of his fingers.

"You smell like vodka," he grunted. "I thought you quit."

Judgmental wanker.

Sneering, I shot back, "And I thought you were dead."

"Well, here I am."

"Yeah, here you are."

We stayed that way, me on the floor with him standing above me like some great harbinger of Death, until he thrust out a hand like he was doing me a service, offering help that I neither wanted nor trusted. I smacked his hand away before rolling onto my knees with a pitiful moan.

All the while, he watched me with inscrutable eyes. "You look like Hell."

"Fuck you, too," I gritted out. He had some nerve walking in here after the shit he'd pulled today. That he'd clearly read my texts but hadn't found me worth the time it took to reply only added fuel to the fire. "Unless you're here to apologize, you can piss right off."

Instead of replying, he walked away. To . . . leave? My alcohol-addled brain tried to compute the fact that he'd moved to the desk that sat beneath the window and was now sifting through the stack of books I'd left out. After months of being stonewalled by him, his curiosity felt like a gross invasion of privacy.

I struggled to my feet. "Did you hear me? I said that unless you're here to apologize, you can piss right—"

"Is that what you want?"

"What?" I queried back, sounding thoroughly hammered. There were currently two Kirills shimmering side by side, but they merged back into one as he turned to rest his arse against the desk. The sight of him there, wearing a worn pair of jeans and a white T-shirt, with the book I'd annotated clutched in one hand—it was too much to take in all at once. I suddenly felt overheated, my skin burning hot with what had to be the onslaught of a fever.

His gaze held mine, unwavering. "Is that what you want? An apology?"

"You don't think I'm owed one?"

Something unmistakably hard flitted through his expression, there and gone again before I could even begin to put my finger on it. When he spoke, it was through clenched teeth. "Owed one as the Volkov heir?"

"Owed one as your best friend, you bloody prick!" I hadn't meant to yell, but now that I'd started, I couldn't seem to shut up. All the worry and hurt from the last nine months poured out of me in a flood of emotion. "Do you know how it felt to wake up and find that you were gone? And not just *gone*. Oh, no. To realize that nobody would tell me where you'd been shipped off to? It took me weeks, Kirill—*weeks*—to learn that you were in Russia. And even then, when I at least could point at a map and say, *He's gone to Moscow*, it was like you became a ghost!"

His Adam's apple bobbed. "Yarik . . ."

"I nearly went mad wondering if you were dead or alive." I wasn't sure when I'd crossed the room, but here I was, caging him in against the desk, hands planted on either side of his hips. Not touching him but still so very, very close to blundering past the one boundary he had, the one I'd always vowed to protect as if it were my own. I was too drunk to be careful. Too drunk to be anything but brutally honest. "I spent nine fucking months waiting for a text, an email, a goddamned carrier pigeon, and you gave me *nothing*. After all that shit you spouted about refusing to let me go, you went and treated me no better than my father ever has."

Unfathomably dark eyes glittered up at me. "Take that back."

"Why should I?" I leaned down so that I could spit venom right in his face when I said, "I'm an embarrassment to you, aren't I? A worthless piece of—"

The book clattered to the floor as Kirill grabbed me by the shirt—

And then he shoved me backward.

He didn't let me go, not when I stumbled over my feet, not when I crashed down onto the bed. Not even when he got close enough to hiss, "You're drunk, Yaroslav. And since I doubt you'll remember any of this tomorrow, I'm going to give you the chance to stop talking before you say something that you'll regret."

Breathing heavily, I propped my weight onto one elbow and slanted my chin upward. "You think I'll regret this?" My jaw went tight, lips firming with all the anger that swept recklessly through my blood. "Tell me, Kiryusha, do *you* regret making me look like a fool?"

It was a direct hit.

I saw the moment he was wounded, how it wept profusely no matter what he did to try and stem the flow. Those beautifully glittering eyes turned anguished, and he released his hold on me, one painstaking finger at a time, to stagger back like I'd actually taken a knife and stabbed him.

I followed, because of course I did, keeping us within short range of each other. "C'mon, tell me. Do you *regret it?*"

In all the years I'd known him, I'd never seen him like this—gaze haunted, voice gone. The thick rug muffled his retreating footfalls, but the rug couldn't disguise his shallow breathing, and I found myself utterly hypnotized by the sight of his rabbiting pulse point just below the jut of his jawline. Of the two of us, I was always the one to follow, but it was me on the hunt this time, me stalking him like prey.

"Do you think you'll sleep tonight?" I purred in a low, furious rasp. "Or do you think that you'll lie awake, the hours ticking by ever-so-slowly, while you remember the look on my face when I tell you that what you did today is *unforgivable?*"

His lips parted.

"But that shouldn't be a problem for you, right?" There was a chill in my bones. Already I felt icy fingers circling my heart. "Because if you've shown me anything in the last nine months, it's that you care more about kissing my father's arse than you ever cared about holding onto me."

With a soft grunt, his back hit the wall beside the door.

And I followed—again. I pressed my hands to the wall above his head and caged him in—again. I lowered my head, cutting the distance between us in half, and spat venom in his face—again.

"I forgive you, you know. For what happened in his study." Tomorrow, I would regret baring my soul. Tomorrow, but not today. "I would withstand a thousand lashes from you. If that's what you needed to survive this world, to save face with my father, I'd hand you the belt, Kiryusha, and I'd let you bleed me dry. But I won't let you be the one to make me feel like I'm worthless. Anyone else," I uttered in a low, trembling voice, "but not you."

I won't survive it.

It would kill me.

An errant tear slipped down my cheek.

I saw the moment he noticed it. The light in his eyes flickered, then went out like the sight of me crying destroyed something vital within him. Then he lifted his hand, fingers already unfurled as if he actually thought to brush away the physical manifestation of my heartache.

Yesterday, if you'd asked me if I would refuse Kirill Volkov the chance to touch me, I would have laughed in your face. Today, all I knew was that I'd shatter into a million little pieces if I let him.

Despite all the vodka, I managed to cleanly evade him.

Grief-stricken, he uttered my name.

"You need to go," I whispered.

There was a time, back when we were kids, when I was utterly obsessed with the idea of seeing my best friend lose control. I remembered lobbing sock-balls at his head and saying every outrageous thing that came to mind, just to push him over the edge. I thought it was what I wanted—what I *craved*.

I was wrong.

Because as it registered that I really was kicking him out, Kirill's entire body hardened like the edge of a steel blade. He stepped forward; this time, I didn't run. With hands that trembled down by my sides, and a gasp that I would deny until my last breath, I let him stand close enough that I swore I could hear his heartbeat.

"You're right, you know," he murmured.

Pulse fluttering, I licked my lips. "About what?"

"I don't sleep."

My gut squirmed uneasily with guilt. "I'm sorry. I shouldn't have said—"

"I don't sleep," he went on gravely, "because your face haunts every one of my nightmares. You may have forgiven me, but I haven't forgiven myself. I see you the way you were that night—the tears on your cheeks, how utterly lifeless you looked when I touched your face."

And then, to my surprise, he did just that.

He fitted his warm, calloused palm to the shape of my cheek with such aching tenderness that renewed tears sprang to my eyes. It was too much. His gentleness. His touch. The fierce understanding that flared in his gaze and pierced me through like an arrowhead. All of it was *too much*.

"Kirill, please," I rasped as hot, cloying *want* washed through me. In a bid for self-preservation, I tried to pull away. "Please, just—"

His palm slid to my nape, holding me captive. "Hate me, Yarik. Tell me I'm a selfish fucking bastard who doesn't deserve to breathe the same air as you." His fingers slid through the strands of my hair. It wasn't on purpose, I didn't think, but it affected me all the same. My heart raced as he used his grip to pull me down so that he could look me dead in the eye when he growled, "But just know that I welcome it, that hatred, because it means that you're *alive*."

My mouth went bone-dry.

It had to be the vodka that made me do it, but I darted

my hand up to lay flat over his, clutching his fingers with mine. The combined weight of our entwined hands at the base of my skull nudged my head down until less than a hairsbreadth separated his lips from mine.

I wanted to taste him.

I wanted to show him that while he'd been sent to Moscow, I'd been right here awaiting his return. Nine months later and the memory of us down by the river still plagued my every waking thought. When we'd been so caught up in a maelstrom of emotions, I thought that he might . . . thought that *we* might—

Kirill's gaze fell to my lips, and then he flinched.

I felt it like an earthquake beneath my feet, a tremor that shouldn't have even registered, but we stood so close, nose to nose, lips millimeters apart, our fingers wound together like braided twine, that it shook me to my core.

Oh, fuck.

Oh, *fuck*—

"I have to go," he said, jerking away, but not before I saw a flash of panic dart across his expression. "I forgot that I have—that there's—" He peered back at me over his shoulder with wide, troubled eyes before shaking his head as if to clear it. "I have to go."

"Wait." I lurched forward, arm stretched out. "Kirill, *wait*—"

But he was already gone.

I was . . . deeply ashamed of what happened next. Of the way panic, rage, and heartbreak tore through me like the wildest of storms until the state of my bedroom too closely resembled the shambled mess that was my soul. There was a fist-shaped hole in the wall and shards of broken glass glittering in the now-damp rug; a wooden chair snapped in two while books littered the floor. And notebook paper strewn—wait.

Those weren't mine.

Still panting from my literal self-destruction, I crawled on my hands and knees over splintered glass to snatch up the closest sheet of paper. The handwriting wasn't mine, but it was . . . familiar.

Too tipsy to make sense of the messy scrawl, I held the paper up to my face. The world around me faded away as I saw the name scribbled at the top.

"No," I whimpered as I scanned the rest. "No, no, no."

Nausea clawed at my throat as I let the letter flutter to the floor, only to grab another and another. Soon, there were so many—with more tucked away inside the pages of the book on constellations I'd annotated—that they fanned out around me in a semi-circle.

I was going to be sick.

Through wet lashes, I stared down at the letter clutched in my fist. It was the first. Dated to just two days after my eighteenth birthday when I'd been frantically trying to gather information on where he'd been sent or if he was even still breathing.

Nine months.

He'd been gone *nine months*, and I had lamented each and every one of those two-hundred-and-seventy-three days. I had thought him dead, and I had thought him an arsehole, but most of all, I'd begged him to write me back.

And he had. Pages and pages worth of letters, so many that it would take me hours just to read them all.

I'd accused Kirill of forgetting me.

He hadn't.

The boy I loved hadn't forgotten me at all.

CHAPTER TWENTY-TWO

KIRILL

20 November 2014

Yarik,

I'm sorry that I've gone. I'm even sorrier that I didn't get the chance to say goodbye. I keep telling myself that it's no different from when I got sent back to England without you. I didn't say bye then, either, if you recall. I figured you knew that I didn't have a choice. But my gut is telling me this time, I should have said something, regardless of whether or not I had a choice.

I didn't.

And if you're wondering why I'm writing you a letter, then I'm sure you can figure out the rest.

Kirill

30 November 2014

Yarik,

Remember that time you got us shipped to an old Soviet prison and tried to make it sound like a five-star accommodation? Well, I'm here to say that things could have been worse. I would choose that moldy fucking room with you over this shit any day.

    Kirill

17 December 2014

Yarik,

Got your message. Thing is, I know you don't give a rat's arse about Moscow, same way I know you've probably typed out a million more texts that you won't ever send.

    You can take some comfort in that, at least.

    If I ever give you these letters, months will have passed, if not years. (I hope not years.) I can't risk putting them in the post. Please understand.

    Kirill

23 January 2015

Yarik,

Your father sent me to St. Petersburg.

He's made the oligarchs nervous. They like him best when they think he exists to serve their every command, like a genie with a bottle—except your father is more likely to murder them in their sleep and then steal their three wishes for himself.

Anyway.

I'm not sure if they're operating on short-sightedness, thinking they'll be the one to tame the Great Petr Volkov (sarcasm), or if they're just so delusional, they don't even realize your father has their every move watched. It would be ironic, maybe, except that I'm the one tasked with doing the watching.

Kirill

4 March 2015

Yarik,

I won't be putting a bullet in your brain. Thought we'd mutually agreed to avoid killing each other?

Kirill

P.S., you don't need luck. You're a pampered prince who can do whatever he wants, remember?

P.P.S., on the subject of you telling me to go

fuck myself—good to know some things haven't changed. ~~You're still a fucking brat.~~

18 March 2015

Yarik,

If I could choose anyone to watch your back while I can't, it would be Daniel Beck. He's reckless and hotheaded but stubbornly loyal. You deserve to have someone stand by your side that you can trust.

~~I'm sorrier than you'll ever know that I broke that trust~~

~~I miss you~~

I hope you're doing all right.

Kirill

3 April 2015

Yarik,

I'm back in Moscow.

Kirill

16 April 2015

Yarik,

Sometimes I wonder what might have come of my life if you hadn't found me. Would I have survived? Or would I have only lived long enough just to end up dead on the street?

Would I have been as lonely without having known you as I am now, stuck halfway around the world with only these letters to keep me sane?

Kirill

7 May 2015

I'm sorry

sorry

yarik forgive me

12 May 2015

Dear Yaroslav,

I've been instructed to transcribe this letter to you on account of my patient, Kirill Volkov. He wishes to let you know that he is healing, but he won't be able to write for a number of days as he isn't sure where he'll end up once leaving the hospital.

He doesn't want you to worry. "Because you will," he's told me to write.

He wants you to know that everything is fine.

From,

Kirill

. . .

13 May 2015

Dear Yaroslav,

This is Dr. Kuznetsova. I debated whether I should write you this letter when I don't have explicit permission from Mr. Volkov, but I wished to let you know that things are not good.

Your friend is a fighter.

He is . . . He is trying. I have never seen anyone try so hard as I have him. When he speaks, it is only your name. When he wakes, he searches the room as if seeking someone who is not there. I suspect he is looking for you.

I wish that I had a number for you or even an email. As I don't, and I don't know what will come of these letters or even Mr. Volkov, I felt it only right that you should know—

He lives for you, Yaroslav.

I hope Death will not catch him.

Best,

Katerina Kuznetsova

20 May 2015

Yaroslav,

Death has not won.

Katerina

. . .

29 June 2015

Yarik,

Every time I put pen to paper, I ask myself whether these letters will ever find their way into your hands. I debate my own transparency. Do I treat them like a diary or like a door to my soul in which only you hold the key?

I don't know.

Right now, I don't know much of anything.

I know that I'm alive. I know that if I wasn't, you'd probably never hear otherwise. The Bratva is a graveyard and we've all been marked for death. You more than most. I know you don't see it, not when your father keeps you on such a tight leash, but these waters are filled with sharks and just the sight of you has them thirsty for blood.

Stay vigilante. Watch your back. ~~I'm worried for you.~~

I hope to see you soon.

Kirill

15 July 2015

Yarik,

I realize that I didn't ever write what happened to me.

I think I'll save that story for when we're together again. Not that you'll know any differently. These pages bear the weight of my consciousness and not a single one has reached your doorstep. I still can't risk putting them in the post to share them with you, but sometimes . . .

Sometimes I wonder if I ever will.
Kirill

21 August 2015
Yarik,
I almost phoned you today.
I want to.
I _need_ to.
Because I knew this day was coming, no matter how often I hoped that it wouldn't. If I reach out to you, he'll know. That'll be worse for you, in the end. Worse than what happened in your father's study. Worse because I promised to stay away, and now he's ordered me to
     I can't even finish that sentence.
     I can't.
     Fuck. _FUCK._

23 August 2015

Yarik,
Answer your bloody fucking phone.

24 August 2015
How many times do I need to fucking ring you before you realize that it's _me_?

25 August 2015
Yarik. What have you done?

26 August 2015
I'm sorry.
I'm sorry for watching.
I'm sorry that I have no other choice.
I'm just so fucking _sorry_

2 September 2015
Yarik,
I don't know if I believe in any sort of after-life. But if it exists, then surely I belong in Hell.

Kirill

10 September 2015
Yarik,
I'm coming home.

CHAPTER TWENTY-THREE

YARIK

It took me three long weeks to get Kirill alone. Even then, we were surrounded by mourners.

And okay, maybe I should have waited until we weren't attending a funeral to corner him, but I was running out of options. Simply put, I was beyond the point of desperation. If this was my one chance to speak with him, then carpe fucking diem. Just let him try and shake me off.

Here goes nothing.

Slanting a nervous glance over my shoulder, I searched the assembly of unfamiliar faces for any sign of my father. When I came up blessedly empty, I drew in a slow, calming breath, then slid silently into the empty spot beside Kirill. Immediately, he stiffened and moved to leave.

"Wait," I uttered pathetically. "Fuck, just *wait*. Please."

Dressed in a black, tailored suit that hugged the firm lines of his body, Kirill remained half in profile, his back to the wall. The width of his shoulders rose with a heavy breath. Then he speared me with his gaze. "We aren't doing this at a funeral."

"Then where? When? You might as well still be in Moscow for all I've seen of you."

"We live in the same house."

"And yet, you're never there."

Shoulders drooping, his shoes tapped soundlessly against the floor as he stepped back into place, though he kept his distance like he wasn't in any hurry to let his guard down. I was so focused on the muscle fluttering in his jaw that I almost missed the way his cheeks had flooded with color.

Wait.

Had he just been avoiding me like I'd suspected? Or had he . . . had he actually been staying somewhere else *with* someone else?

The thought almost knocked me back onto my arse. Had the chairs not been reserved for the frail and elderly, I would have sat down, just to withstand the unwanted visual of Kirill with—with *someone*—assaulting me. Grappling for control over my expression, I forced my closed fists behind my back like a toddler being told to sit on their hands to stop them from playing with fire.

Only problem was, I wanted nothing more than to dance amidst the flames.

Did you forget? He ran *from you. And by the looks of it, he wants nothing more than to keep on running.*

Maybe I'd had the right of it, striking up conversation with him in the middle of a funeral. It meant that I couldn't make a scene, no matter how badly I wanted to pepper him with questions. Jealousy writhed inside me like a living, breathing beast. Gritting my teeth, I flicked my aimless gaze over the ornate, gold-plated icons that decorated the muraled walls of the Russian Orthodox Cathedral. It was the oldest of its kind in London. I'd been baptized here. Buried my mother here, too, on church grounds. And while I wasn't particularly religious, I still pitched my voice respectfully low as I'd been taught to do from birth. "We both know you've been avoiding me."

Kirill stared straight ahead. The muscle in his jaw ticked faster. "I'm not."

"You are."

"Yarik, I'm not playing these games—"

"It's fine if you have been; I don't blame you. But here's the thing"—I spared him a single, vulnerable glance—"you mean something to me. No," I corrected with a quick, emphatic shake of my head, "you mean *everything* to me. And I said bloody awful things to you."

If I thought his body couldn't grow any stiffer, I was immediately proven wrong. His knuckles turned bone-white just before he slipped them into the front pockets of his trousers. "Let's not do this here. Please."

If it were up to him, we'd never do this at all.

Meanwhile, I was slowly unraveling.

I'd once heard that apologies aren't for the injured party so much as they're given to wipe clean a guilty conscience. If that logic held true, then the only reason I'd showed up here today—for the death of some foot soldier I didn't even know—was for purely selfish reasons. It made me uncomfortable to think I was using the loss of someone's life for my own benefit, but the idea of going yet another day without getting any of this off my chest was unbearable.

I had to believe that Kirill needed to hear the words just as badly as I needed to say them.

"We *have* to do this, don't you see?" Giving up all

pretenses, I hunched my shoulders to draw less attention to myself. Inadvertently, my elbow pressed into his sternum. While he didn't pull away, his cautious gaze flinched up to meet mine. That brief, shared glance elicited a tremor down my spine. I plowed on. It was now or never. "In your letters, you wrote that you haven't forgiven yourself for what happened last year—but, Kirill, I can't forgive myself for what I said just three weeks ago."

The somber silence around us was crudely interrupted as the archpriest began the service.

Lowering my voice even more, I let raw heartache rasp across my tongue. "I was angry and upset. You were gone and I . . . I was a mess." I raked my fingers through my hair, my eyes darting hastily over the people around us. I shifted closer. "I'd just spent nine months terrified you were never coming back, and then you did, in my father's shadow, no less, looking perfect and untouchable, like you didn't have a single care in the world, and I lost it, Kiryusha. I wanted to hurt you as badly as you hurt me."

Except that he'd already been hurt, almost fatally so. The thought that I could have just as easily been attending *his* funeral today nearly dropped me to my knees.

"I'm sorry. With everything I am, I'm so, so sorry."

Unable to resist any longer, I twisted away from the congregation so that the only person filling my vision was Kirill. Reading his letters had consumed my entire being. I kept them in the annotated book he'd slipped them into, and the thin pages were already becoming worn from my constant handling.

He'd never given me such unfettered access to his thoughts before.

His mind was . . . addicting, *gut-wrenching*. Insomnia had become my second-closest friend, after Kirill himself, because no matter what I did, I couldn't erase the terrifying prospect that he could have died, and I never would have known. He wrote that he worried about me, and yet I was surrounded by bodyguards every second of the day to the point of suffocation—I'd practically had to browbeat Anton into waiting for me outside the cathedral just so I could have this conversation without him eavesdropping.

But what about Kirill?

Where were his guards? Who ensured his security?

Like every other foot soldier in the Bratva, he only had himself. The difference was, of course, that Kirill spent his life teetered across two worlds. Within the social hierarchy of Father's army, he was at the bottom. And yet, he lived with us, ate with us, *slept* with us, under my father's own roof.

When he'd said that he didn't have a choice, he'd meant it.

He was surviving the only way he knew how, and I had twisted the last nine months of deafening silence to make it all about me—the privileged, spoiled mafia prince who never had to worry about whether he'd live or die. Unless, of course, it was at the hands of my own father.

Be grateful I don't put you down like a dog.

It wasn't the same. And I felt such terrible shame, knowing that I had stuck Kirill between a rock and a hard place, expecting unconditional loyalty from him when I offered nothing in return. What did I even have to give him? My friendship? *Love*? Fucking worthless, just like I was.

Loyalty to my father guaranteed him safety.

He deserved that. It was the bare minimum, really.

The sensation of a shoulder gently nudging my arm snapped me back to reality, drawing my attention down to Kirill's upturned face. His brows were furrowed, his head tipped back so that he could hold my gaze. I expected him to pull away so we were no longer touching, but then the middle-aged man on the other side of him jostled toward us, leaving Kirill no wriggle room to escape.

I wanted him.

Fuck, I wanted him so badly that my *teeth* ached.

I stepped back, anyway, giving him breathing room. I wanted him, yes, but I loved him more. I loved him enough that I would bury these unwanted feelings of mine to the depths of my core. Forever, if I had to.

"I'm sorry, too," he finally said. When I lifted a brow, he seemed to shore himself up to get the words out before he lost his nerve. "I was the one who told Volkov what you were up to with Robert Murray."

Oh. Weakly, I tried for a smile. "It's okay."

"I was the one who had them all monitored. The one who *did* the monitoring."

Those weren't the normal duties of a foot soldier, and I felt my stomach churn uneasily. "It's okay, Kiryusha. Really."

"And I've watched you, too."

It was, I thought, as if the floor had opened up beneath me. I would have been in freefall, but Kirill's midnight eyes kept me tethered to this church, to the archpriest's monotone sermon and the sweet scent of incense permeating the air. At the base of my spine, my fingers knotted together so tightly that circulation loss had to be imminent.

"Everything you do," Kirill confessed roughly, "I see. Everything you say, I hear."

I struggled to find my voice. "What do you do with that information?"

But I knew.

Fuck, I *knew,* and the way he watched me now, with remorse and self-loathing warring in his distraught gaze . . . Well, it was all the confirmation I needed. He hadn't been avoiding me for the last three weeks because he'd been angry with me. He'd avoided me out of *guilt.*

"Right." I jerked my gaze away, vision blurring. "Okay."

It wasn't okay. Maybe I hadn't had much freedom to begin with, but it was still something, at least, to know that if I tried hard enough, I could escape for a few hours of solitary bliss. Now there was no part of my life that my father wouldn't have full access to.

I was a prisoner.

Chained to the future Volkov throne the way Princess Andromeda had been chained to a rock as a sacrifice to the sea monster, Cetus. But instead of being rescued by Perseus and his trusty steed, Pegasus, as Andromeda had been in the Greek myth Kirill had once told me about, my own savior had opted to save himself. *Survival in the only way he knows,* I reminded myself. If only I loved him a little less, maybe I would hate him for it.

Gruffly, I asked, "Do you remember when Pavel died?"

Kirill's nod was almost imperceptible.

"I wondered if it was better to know the person you killed, and you said it was worse knowing the way that you knew Pavel." The flesh of my palms screamed from the biting pressure of my nails. "I don't agree."

"Yarik, I—"

"It's better to know the truth," I interjected sharply, "no matter how much it hurts." Tension crackled like a livewire between us. At some point, we'd shifted to stand shoulder to shoulder, both of us looking out into the assembly of mourners. Inside my soul, it felt like I was dying, too. "How many cameras?"

There was a slight pause as if he was struggling for an answer, before he finally admitted in a flat, emotionless voice, "Throughout the house."

"My bedroom?"

"Yes."

Trying not to think about all the times I'd potentially jerked off in my room, I forced myself to adopt the same impassive inflection he had. "Anton?"

"He wears a body camera."

"And you?" I ground my teeth, wanting desperately to look at him, to gauge the truth in his eyes, but I held myself unnaturally still, unwilling to let my self-control shatter. "Are you wearing a camera right now?"

Another pause.

Then, hoarsely, "Yes."

"This tape. Will you give it to him?"

"No."

For the first time in my life, I didn't believe him.

My right palm split open, the flesh finally surrendering as it broke. There'd be blood. Maybe a small scar to match the ones he'd left on my back. I often thought that I loved Kirill Volkov so much that it hurt. And yet, with the damning truth laid out before us, I realized with a dawning sense of horror that I felt nothing at all.

I was numb, hollowed out. Like an ancient tree on the cusp of death.

In a voice like gravel, Kirill rasped, "I don't want to lose you."

"You won't," I vowed.

It was a lie.

We were already lost.

PART FIVE
LONDON, ENGLAND

CHAPTER TWENTY-FOUR

YARIK

On paper, I'd become the perfect mafia darling.

I schemed.

I killed.

I prospered.

No one could ask anything more of me because, at twenty-one, I gave all of myself to the Bratva. To everyone's surprise, including my father's, I sat at his side like a prizted stallion. Hand over a crown and I could have easily played the part of a god. *Bow down to me. Crawl to me. Worship me.* No one dared tell me no because I was Yaroslav Volkov, heir to the Volkov empire, favored prince to all.

That was the problem with perfection.

It glittered and glowed, alluring as gold. But far beneath the surface, I was rotten down to my core.

I hated.

I envied.

I *wanted*.

And I did it all with every fiber of my fucking soul.

"Here." Ale sloshed over the rim of a pint glass as Beck

set it down in front of me. "Don't know how you drink this shit. Tastes like piss."

"Maybe I enjoy not being a stereotype."

When his red-rimmed gaze dropped to the Beluga Noble he'd ordered, humor flirted at the corner of his mouth. "Maybe I like putting hair on my chest."

"Yeah? Maybe consider abstaining. Yours is already liable to be mistaken for a rug."

"Women like it, boss. I wouldn't want to disappoint them." As if to prove his point, he downed the rest of the expensive, Russian-label vodka in one smooth go. His fifth or sixth shot of the evening. Drunk bastard looked downright joyful when he teased, "A virgin like you wouldn't understand."

It took everything in my power to keep my gaze from flinching away.

But the baby hairs on my nape still stood on end, and I was desperate for it—to look over my shoulder toward the long, dimly lit hallway that led from the beating heart of the nightclub to the toilets. Some American song throbbed over the speakers, and everywhere I looked, bodies swayed and gyrated like tangled reeds caught in a wayward breeze. I'd be expected to get out there soon. Find some pretty girl to dance with, maybe even kiss.

My men expected it.

Father expected it.

A mafia darling schemed and killed and prospered, but above all, he *fucked*.

Beck reached for my pint glass and took a swig. This far into the night, he never really cared whether ale actually tasted like piss. It was all the same going down. Still puckered his lips like a teenager after their first taste of booze, though. "You aren't saving it, are you?"

The devil on my shoulder demanded my surrender.

Turn. Look. Watch.

"Saving what?" I forced myself to ask, my gaze bouncing from Beck to Eren, who had his tongue down a girl's throat as blue and purple strobe lights painted neon streaks over their writhing bodies. There was a frenetic energy in the air tonight. I'd felt it the moment we walked in. But I was safe—or safe enough, at any rate—so long as I played the game.

"Your virginity." Listing sideways, Beck dropped his chin onto an upturned palm. "Always wanted to ask but figured it ain't any of my business."

"Then why ask now?"

Beck grinned at me. "Because I give zero fucks, mate, that's why. Anyway. Tell Daddy Beck the truth, yeah? You savin' yourself for marriage?"

Despite my father's continued ambitions for me, I had no plans to marry.

Not now, not ever.

"No. And don't ever call yourself 'Daddy Beck' again. Fucking hell."

"Hmm." Beck sipped more of my ale. "Well, are you waiting for *the one*?"

Turn. Look. Watch.

It took herculean effort to scoff, "The *one*? Jesus, don't tell me you actually believe in soulmates."

"Me?" Beck barked out a laugh, too far gone to notice that I didn't join in. "I believe in them, all right. One for each night of the week." Leaning across the table, he clapped a hand on my shoulder. "Come on, go out there and get your prick wet. I can play rank for the night." He hoisted himself up a little, spine snapping straight. "Beck, stop drinking. Eren, put your dick away. Kirill—"

"You need a muzzle."

"It wouldn't help." With a sigh, he slumped down onto the table, head bent over his clasped hands as if in prayer. "God, please forgive Yarik for not using what You gave him. What a tragic waste. A dictragedy. Dick-ragedy? Anyway, what I wouldn't do to be blessed with a cock the size of—"

"All right. You're done for the night."

"But I'm not done praying."

"Keep it up and the only prayer you'll be making is when my foot is so far up your arse, you're speaking in tongues. Come on." I hauled him up by the back of his shirt, which was no small feat considering he outweighed me by at least two stone and stood almost half a head taller. Over his shoulder, I made eye contact with Eren, who nodded back at me before peeling himself away from the girl with a wink and a dimpled grin. When he got close, I thrust Beck in his direction. "Watch him, would you?"

"Eren the Nanny. Put that on my gravestone when I die." Grumbling aside, he grasped Beck by the nape, keeping him close since we both knew he'd make a run for it, given the chance. Daddy Beck was a chaotic twat. Sober Beck would never.

Eren's questioning gaze flicked toward the hallway. "Kirill?"

My stomach turned over. "I've got him."

What little beer I'd had sloshed in my belly as I put one foot in front of the other, my bodyguard, Anton, an ever-present shadow trailing a few steps behind me. I hated these nights out. Hated what they stood for, hated that I couldn't get out of them. Most of all, I hated that I needed them like a man of the cloth needs his flock. Without them . . .

A shudder whispered down my spine.

This was about survival. Point-blank. It was about the fact that I was watched twenty-four-seven, and if I had any hope of keeping my head attached to my shoulders, then I had to keep up the pretense that I was exactly the sort of mafia prince expected to one day take my father's throne.

Ruthless. Straight. Perfect.

Sometimes, when I was drowning in a thick, oily vat of envy, I let myself imagine the thrill of the chase. Locking eyes with someone across a darkened room. Desire unfurling in my gut like wisps of smoke; inhibitions crumbling in the face of temptation like a sailor unable to deny the sweet lure of a siren song. Bodies colliding, hot mouths meeting. A possessive hand gripping the back of my neck, hauling me so close that I felt every hard ridge, every shallow breath, desperate for more, begging for the chance to—

Anton stepped forward to open the door to the toilets. "Petrovich, let me."

"I've got it." He'd been with me for years but still made a point to use the patronymic form of my name. He said that it was out of respect. I'd told him, more than once, that it wasn't necessary. The constant reminder that I was my father's son only made me want to stab something—preferably my father. When Anton didn't move out of the way, I dragged in a slow inhale. "*Ponyal*, Anton."

His lips thinned. "We've been over this. I'm meant to go where you go. Your father—"

"My father isn't here," I said sharply before scrambling to mask my impatience with a friendly grin. "Let me tell you a little secret . . ." Ducking my head, I leaned in. "I don't need help pissing. Think I've got that biological talent covered."

He pinched his mouth shut in disgust.

Anton Kotov was not my friend. He was loyal to the Volkov name, one of many on my father's payroll. A few years ago, he accidentally let it slip that he viewed his duties to me as one step above scrubbing shit stains from a toilet. He hadn't apologized for the insult—not that I'd expected one—and the only reason he didn't quit was because my father paid him a small fortune to spy on me. Secretly, of course. Thanks to Kirill, I knew all about the little body cameras he wore.

Which was the only reason why these nights out happened at all.

Go back to your king and tell him lies about his only son—

Ruthless. Straight. Perfect.

It took everything in me not to scream.

Anton's dark brown gaze went to the door. "I'll wait here, then."

You do that, I almost sneered.

"Cheers, mate," is what came out of my mouth instead, because Yaroslav Volkov was only ruthless when the situation called for it and never when his actions might be mistaken for disobedience. "Be out in a minute."

This far down the hall, near the club's back exit, the concrete floor still throbbed beneath my feet, but the music was less intense, muffled. Quiet enough to hear the tail end of a moan slip out from the lavatory behind me.

Fuck.

Pulse skipping, I turned my back on Anton before he had the chance to change his mind, then cracked the door open with the toe of my Oxford and closed it immediately behind me, cursing myself even as I pressed my back to the solid wood. What did it matter if Anton saw? If the whole bloody *world* saw?

Kirill was allowed this.

He was—he *was*, and I had to accept that—

Another moan, this one low, guttural. His. I kept my head down but allowed my gaze to lift from the polished leather of my shoes to the mirror opposite me. I saw her first. Down on her knees, crushed-velvet skirt hiked up around her waist, black-painted fingernails frantic as they worked between her thighs. She was blonde, like me. Just a coincidence, though. He'd fucked women with hair every shade under the sun. But tonight, she was blonde.

It felt like a dagger to the heart.

There was blood spilling out, had to be. So much of it that even if I had a needle and thread, there'd be no sewing up the wound fast enough to keep from bleeding out. I tried to breathe through the debilitating ache of envy, and pain, and want. Tried so fucking, *fucking* hard, but I remained short of breath, still plastered to the door like I might actually find the strength to walk away.

I didn't.

I wasn't sure that I ever would.

So, I submerged myself in the envy—pain—want, drowning evermore, and forced myself to acknowledge that the blonde was on her knees because the man I loved was fucking her mouth.

Her lips were red.

Maybe from lipstick. Maybe from all the enthusiastic sucking.

You shouldn't be here.

Common sense said that I should leave. I'd expected

to walk in and find him finishing—not metaphorically, either, but literally wrapping things up with a *thanks-for-that-see-you-never* expression on his face before he strode out the door like he hadn't come down someone's throat just minutes beforehand.

It was the way he usually handled things.

Not that he disappeared for sex very often—once or twice a year, if that. To a virgin like me, who once stupidly believed that we'd be each other's firsts, even that felt like too much. Here was my wretched truth: a best friend would let him carry on. Hell, even a mediocre friend would guard the door, maybe offer a high-five when he finished. *Great job, mate. So bloody happy for you.*

I wasn't a good friend.

On the few occasions when he did slip away for a shag, I told myself—fine, I *lied* to myself—that he wouldn't care if he saw me lingering nearby, waiting for him to be done, because these hookups were just that, rare, impersonal opportunities for him to relieve stress.

He didn't take them home.

He didn't take them out either.

He fucked them in backend alleys or nightclub bathrooms, or wherever else he brought them that got the message across that there wouldn't be any repeats.

There should have been some comfort in that, knowing that he never saw them again. And maybe there would have been if our already strained friendship hadn't grown so cold. The boy whom I'd saved from the river had turned to ice, and I had no idea how to thaw him out. Nothing I did worked. Nothing I said softened him. Even when he fucked, like he did now, he seemed to find no joy in it.

The blonde whimpered, her head bobbing faster.

Leave. Right. Now.

Clearly, there wasn't a shred of morality still left in my bones because I dragged my gaze upward, away from the blonde on her knees, hoping for just a glimpse of him. And when I didn't get it from where I stood by the door, I tossed all sanity aside and stepped closer to the duo, taking advantage of the partition wall that separated the stalls from a row of sinks.

My heart pounded in my ears.

This was a betrayal of trust. An invasion of privacy. I wasn't *welcome* here. And yet, for better or worse, I hated and envied and *wanted*, and like the pitifully weak bastard that I was, I devoured the sight of him even as it killed me.

He was fully clothed. Trousers unzipped, his dress shirt still unbuttoned, except for the very top two that he always left undone. The soft, black fabric hugged the strong lines of his torso, same as it did the corded muscles of his arms, which he'd lifted above his head to grip the top of the stall. *At least he's not touching her* bitterly crossed my mind. Further consolation, if consolation were a prize. Which it wasn't.

Because this voyeuristic view was all I'd ever have of him.

A rumble of pleasure reverberated in his chest.

The blonde had pulled her fingers away from her clit to wrap around his shaft. Below the waist they were all shadows, thanks to my new vantage point, but I heard the damp grip of her palm stroking him nice and slow; saw the way his heavy lids fluttered closed as a flush crested his cheeks.

My breathing came a little faster.

"Like this?" the blonde asked eagerly. "I want to make

you feel good." The ends of her long hair teased the swell of her arse as she tipped her head back, seeking eye contact, I was sure, which Kirill didn't return. He only gripped the stall with straining fingers, keeping his distance even while he had this woman down on her knees.

It was a jarring juxtaposition I hadn't expected.

I'd thought the sex would be hot, and it was, in the sense that it was all about getting off, but it also wasn't—aside from the obvious stimuli, he seemed completely closed off from reality. Like the blonde kneeling at his feet didn't exist. Did he even want this? Did he even *like* it?

It was a shocking revelation, one I wasn't sure had registered to the blonde who was all but begging for scraps of his affection.

Years ago, I might have pestered him into opening up, but there was an invisible wall between us now, and no matter how hard I worked to scale the jagged rocks, they only seemed to grow ever taller. One of these days, there wouldn't even be a ladder to climb, and I'd be forced to break the damn wall down, stone by stone, or risk being left behind.

Wrong as it was, I couldn't tear my gaze away from the mirror.

Couldn't tear my gaze away from *him*.

His jaw clenched. Plush, peach lips thinned. There was a flash of something—frustration, maybe, or impatience—bleeding into his expression just before it all blanked out behind a mask of gruff indulgence. He must have realized that he had to give her *something* because he lowered one hand to ghost over the top of her head. I watched, enthralled, as he wrapped her long, blonde hair around his fingers, then fisted the strands, tight, at the base of her skull.

The dominant gesture jerked her head back so he filled her entire vision.

"Tighten your fist." The gravel-pitched words were torn from his throat, his midnight-black eyes still squeezed shut. "Good girl. Now spit on the head."

Fuck.

Fuck.

Fuck—

"Slick your palm for me," he ordered huskily, "keep me wet. Like that, love. Just like that."

It was an illusion.

All of it.

The endearment, the sinful approval on his handsome face, the way he touched her hair, guiding her mouth down over him. None of it was real. Just a sensual, fabricated lie to get him over the finish line.

So, tell me why I was swept up in the fantasy. Tell me why my hand was shaking as I pressed it to the wall beside me because it was either that or press it to the front of my jeans, where my dick had gone rock hard. Tell me why I was standing here watching my best friend get head through a reflection in the mirror, wishing I was the one on my knees for him when he didn't even want *her*.

But the twisted lies he wove had already trapped me in their gossamer strands.

In my mind's eye, *I* was the one he wanted. The floor was hard and unforgiving beneath my knees, but I welcomed the sting just as I welcomed the sensation of short, crisp hairs teasing my palms as I dragged his trousers down past his thighs to his knees. Because I wasn't like the blonde, docile and overeager to please.

I wanted Kirill Volkov at my mercy.

I wanted to shatter his control even as he punished me for driving him to the brink of madness.

And he *would* punish me—with his fingers gripping the short, wavy strands of my hair, shoving my face so close to his prick that the mushroomed head grazed my parted lips. I wanted a taste. I wanted *him.*

"Now spit on the head," he'd growl, just as he had to the blonde, and I'd tease him with the promise of what he wanted—the tip of my tongue dipping into his slit, moaning as I licked up a pearl of pre-cum—but I'd give him nothing more until he had no choice but to open his eyes and meet my hungry gaze. Only when we were locked in a battle of the wills, with lust crackling between us, would I finally surrender.

I'd spit on the head of his dick.

I'd swallow him to the back of my throat.

I'd use one hand to stroke him and the other to grip his arse, so even though I was the one kneeling, choking on his length, he'd feel my nails digging into his flesh for days after, a reminder that it was *me* who made him feel this way, who made him come undone.

The reverie crashed and burned around me as the sounds of sloppy sucking reached my ears.

I had one hand on the wall, the other against my fly. Before I could stop myself, I was rolling my hips into my palm, seeking relief when there was none to be had. Not on this side of the wall. Not when I wasn't the one he wanted, not even for a quick, meaningless fuck in a public bathroom.

And yet, I was too far gone to stop.

Biting my bottom lip to keep quiet, I fixated on the

sound of his ragged breathing as well as the rhythmic creak of wood under his ever-tightening grip on the stall.

He looked fucking beautiful.

The muscles in his exposed forearm flexed as he adjusted his hold on the blonde. She was moaning keenly now, using both hands, it seemed, to stroke him while her head bobbed faster and faster, the brutal pace set by Kirill himself.

His eyes stayed shut.

Meanwhile, praise dripped from his lying, deceitful tongue—things like, "Fuck, yes, that's it," or "Goddamn it, love, you feel so good," and there I was, one second away from unzipping my jeans and jacking off where he could see me, if only he bothered to look.

It was a terrible thing, wishing for a Hell you know that you'd never survive.

Still, like a masochist, I stayed.

How long until he noticed that they weren't alone? How long until he saw the truth in my gaze, that I wished that he might look at me, really, truly *look* at me, even just once? Long enough to see that I cared far more than I should, that I would cut out my heart and lay it down at his feet, if only he'd let me.

In the end, Fate had other plans.

The door behind me swung open and I panicked— exactly as I had that long-ago day in the woods when my classmate and his girl caught me watching them together. I spun away before I had the chance to second-guess my decision, roughly shouldering the stranger out of the way without an apology—because I couldn't risk Kirill hearing me speak.

I couldn't risk him *hating me.*

• • •

I was wrong for this.

Wrong to crave him the way I did, wrong to hurry up to my room as soon as I got home, slam the door shut behind me, and wrestle with my fly the minute I was alone. I stumbled in the darkness, knocked into my wardrobe, and sent items scattering to the floor.

Glass shattered.

I was too busy shoving my jeans down to mid-thigh to give a fuck.

Desire rode me hard as I planted one hand on top of the now-bare wardrobe, then spat in my other as makeshift lube before wrapping it around my stiff length. I had to squeeze the base, hard, just to keep from coming.

I could hear him, even now.

The low groans, the tapered moans. The way he'd brought himself to the edge, over and over again, never relinquishing enough control to lose himself in the bliss of oblivion. Given the chance, I would have gotten him there. Or maybe not—maybe I would want it to last, so I'd drag his orgasm out until he gritted his teeth, wordlessly demanding that I let him come.

Yeah.

That was exactly it—I would never stop looking at his face, watching his features twist with anguish like it physically hurt him each time I forced him to wait a little longer. Call me a bastard, a sadist, but all I wanted was to see my best friend *beg*.

"Fuck," I panted hotly. "Fuck, fuck, *fuck*."

My touch was all rough friction, even with spit to ease the way, but I'd be damned if I stopped now. I had to come. I *had* to. Letting my head hang low, I breathed hard through my nose as I stroked even faster.

The fantasy sucked me right back under.

How his Adam's apple might bob every time I dodged another one of his commands—*suck harder, tongue my slit, cup my balls.* How his pupils would swallow his irises, his full, tempting lips parting on a bitten-off grunt when he finally—*finally*—lost control and used his grip on my hair to make me choke on his dick.

My hips were punching forward now, chasing my fist the way Kirill would ruthlessly chase the release only I could give him. Desperation lined with dread. Like whatever followed after would never be as good as the thrill of the ride. Sweat beaded my nape. I was suddenly grateful for the darkness, for the privacy it provided from the cameras stationed throughout the room. Whenever I jerked off, I hid in the shower. But I couldn't pull away from Fantasy Kirill—

His lean hips rolling as he thrusted into my mouth, his gaze glittering down at me with surprise as much as it shone with need.

I want you, that look said, and I almost fucking lost it.

I bit my lip so hard that I was surprised when I didn't draw blood. The sound of desperate wanking reverberated in the otherwise silent room. Shallow breathing. Long groans and stifled whimpers. I paused long enough to lick a stripe across my palm, and then there was only the *thwack-thwack-thwack* of my tight fist shuttling over my cock, twisting roughly at the swollen head the way I liked before sinking back down to the root.

"Yarik," he'd say right there at the end—not a plea at that point but a gritty command. To put him out of his misery and end it all. And because I was merciful, I'd lead him right over the edge, soaking in every undulation of his hips, moaning around his cock as he came in spurts on my tongue. Unable to pull away just yet, I'd stay balanced on my knees while I licked him clean.

Me and him.

Him and me.

Except that I was alone in the dark. Alone with a fantasy, an illusion that wasn't real and never would be, and when I came, I was just as alone as I'd been in that nightclub, hidden behind a wall. There was no one around to hear me whimper Kirill's name, no one to clean me up afterward. Just cum spattered across a piece of furniture that I'd ignore until tomorrow because my heart suddenly felt too raw to do anything but twist into a painful knot.

Slowly, I sank to the floor.

Tears pricked at the backs of my eyes as the truth unraveled before me—for the first time that I could remember, he'd actually gone home with someone, nodding his goodbye to me while I stood with Beck and Eren outside the club. An ugly laugh burrowed in my chest before clawing its way free.

I was the perfect mafia darling.

I schemed.

I killed.

I prospered.

And I fucked, all right. I fucked my fist each and every night, wishing my best friend would love me the way that I so desperately still loved him.

CHAPTER TWENTY-FIVE

YARIK

"We're all good for tomorrow," Eren said as he lowered into the chair adjacent to mine a few days later, his brown eyes still fixed on the phone in his hand. Even from here, I could see that he had his favorite calendar app pulled up on the screen. The man lived for a perfectly plotted schedule. I figured it was a leftover habit from his army days. "Flight is booked, and—"

"Tell me again why we aren't flying private?"

I stared at Beck, who was lazily toying with a trench knife by tossing it up into the air like a juggler with a death wish. "Because my father hates you, that's why."

"Hates me?" Somehow, the crazy bastard managed to catch the blade by the tip without severing a finger, only to flip it around, so that he could playfully thrust the pointed edge in my direction. "How about hates *you*, my liege?"

"I think I'm the only one here that he doesn't hate." Beck and I both glanced at Eren, who still hadn't bothered to lift his head from his phone to fully join the conversation. His dark brown hair hung in coiled ringlets in front of his face. When three seconds passed without either me or Beck speaking, he finally blew one thick curl out of his eyes. "What?" He set his phone down on the kitchen table. "He can't hate me when he doesn't even know me."

"He definitely hates you," I said bluntly.

"Thanks to forced proximity," Beck tacked on. He pointed the knife at Eren. "Forced proximity with us, I mean, not with the Sperm Donor."

Eren's nose wrinkled. "Should you really be calling the *pakhan* that?"

"Well, I'm not calling him *Daddy*, if that's what you're gettin' at."

"I wasn't. I really, really wasn't."

"That's right. Because there's only one daddy here, mates, and it's yours truly." When Beck waved a hand— the one clutching the knife—in front of his body, Eren turned to me with a half-crazed look that said he was about five seconds away from putting a bullet in Beck's skull.

Struggling to hold back a laugh, I cleared my throat. "So, flight's booked. And Marchetti, where are we meeting him?"

Relief chased away the lingering irritation in his gaze as Eren went back to his beloved calendar. "We'll get into Naples around noon. I've booked us a reservation at Marchetti's favorite trattoria. Hopefully, that will soften him up before we break the news."

Beck snorted. "Have you met Dante Marchetti? Cold bastard wouldn't melt an ice lolly even if you shoved it up his arse."

With a defeated sigh, Eren's eyes slid closed. "Do you

ever listen to yourself? Like, really, truly *listen* to yourself?”

“Every day of my life, mate.” Beck offered him a wolfish grin. “And aren’t you one lucky cunt, getting to hear the sound of my voice for the rest of your life.”

“Just kill me. Please,” Eren muttered, although to whom, I wasn’t even sure.

The three of us had been together for the better part of four years, and while there’d been plenty of times when I felt like an exhausted parent herding a pair of constantly squabbling children, I’d never . . . Well, aside from Kirill, I’d never had any friends at all. Beck and Eren were it for me, though in many ways, there was still so much that I kept hidden from them.

Like the fact that I was gay.

It wasn’t something that I planned on telling them. Much as I’d like to think that they wouldn’t care, there wasn’t any point in testing the waters. For as long as I existed in the Bratva, I’d be tracked like prey, my every move watched and recorded. Anton, my father’s brigadiers, *Kirill*—they all had me locked in their sights with no hope of ever breaking free.

I swallowed, tightly, then subtly lowered my gaze to my phone, which I had balanced on my thigh. With a flick of my fingers, I pulled up my most recent texts—still nothing.

It was starting to feel like I’d gotten away with murder.

Kirill’s absence since the club was either a blessing or a curse; I just wasn’t sure which one yet. Either way, it seemed that I’d have another few days to sweat out the rest of my shame while we were roasting in the warm Italian sun.

Good luck trying to forget the memory of him leaving with her.

I put my phone facedown on the table, my stomach twisting with bitter jealousy.

"Marchetti isn't going to like hearing that his older brother's cut him off," I said, drawing Beck and Eren's attention back to me and away from each other. "That's not our problem. We're not there to get involved in family drama. Either he agrees to open his own contract with us or he's done. Obviously, the hope is the former."

"Or the Sperm Donor will get very, very angry."

Eren rolled his eyes at Beck. To me, he said, "Can we leave him behind? I'm begging you."

Him being Daniel Beck.

I cracked a smile. "You have my blessing to smother him in his sleep on the flight home."

"You are a true hero," Eren utterly dryly, just as Beck exclaimed, "Oi! I'm right here, ain't I? Don't be talkin' like I can't hear the two of you."

Whatever he said next was drowned out by the buzz of white noise in my ears as a familiar body entered my periphery. I turned my head slightly, already knowing whom I'd find.

Kirill.

He was standing just inside the front door of Beck's flat with one hand tucked casually into the pocket of his trousers while he spoke quietly with Anton. Just the sight of him there—completely unexpected since I hadn't realized he even knew where Beck lived—was enough to short-circuit my brain.

I wanted to throw myself at him while simultaneously wanting to hurl my guilt-ridden body from the closest window.

Fuck.

Beck's good humor faded as he noticed Kirill. "What's he doing here?"

Wondering the same, I went for nonchalance—and failed. My heart thrashed wildly against my rib cage as I wet my lips. "Don't know. I didn't invite him."

Even Eren peered over his shoulder, watching with wary eyes as Anton nodded at whatever Kirill told him before slipping out into the hallway beyond Beck's flat. My best friend left the front door open as he turned toward where we sat in the kitchen. Beside me, Beck shifted his weight, rising to his feet as though he could personally withstand whatever Kirill was about to throw at us.

I pushed to my feet, too.

Truthfully, I didn't blame Beck or Eren for their hesitation when it came to Kirill. He regularly spent time with us, like the other night at the club, but no one was blind to the fact that in the last three years, Kirill had slowly, mercilessly, climbed the ladder until he had a permanent seat at my father's table as his bookkeeper, or *kassir*. Sometimes, the only time Kirill came around was to collect money that would go directly into my father's coffers or be strategically placed into the hands of people who would otherwise see the Volkov empire fall.

Beck and Eren liked Kirill, I knew they did, but they didn't trust him.

It killed me that some days I felt the same way.

"Hey," I said, cutting around the table until I stood directly before him. Despite the unease swimming in my gut over his unexpected arrival, the pathetic eagerness with which I met his gaze was all too genuine. I was weak for him, and it didn't seem to matter what wrongs he committed against me—there was still nothing I loved more than existing in his orbit. "I didn't realize you were stopping by." Carefully, I glanced over his shoulder to the open doorway. "Did Anton get bad news?"

Did you *bring bad news?* I bit the question back before it escaped.

"Your father wanted me to pass a message along. It couldn't wait."

A private message that wasn't for Anton's spying ears? The unease swimming in my gut multiplied tenfold. I wasn't naïve enough to think that Kirill had rushed all this way to tell me some clandestine secret of my father's, but I still heard myself ask Beck and Eren if they'd mind giving us a few minutes alone. It was a testament to his loyalty that Beck didn't complain about being kicked out of his own flat—just squeezed my shoulder as he headed for the door.

The *snick* of the lock turning over echoed like a foghorn in my ears. *Habit,* I thought, as Beck closed up, too busy bickering with Eren to realize locking us in here wasn't exactly necessary. And not that we couldn't just walk out whenever we wanted to. Soon, their voices faded into silence.

Kirill stepped away.

I watched him go, never taking my eyes off him. The stiff way he held his shoulders . . . "Something's wrong. What is it?"

Instead of answering, he shrugged out of his jacket to reveal a gray, long-sleeved dress shirt that he paused to cuff at the elbows. The jacket he draped over the closest chair.

Sometimes, it was a shock to see my best friend all grown up. Somewhere in his mid-twenties, the Kirill

Volkov I'd fallen for was nowhere to be found. In his place was a man with battle-weary eyes that missed absolutely nothing. The angular jaw was perfectly clean-shaven, the shoulders strong enough to carry the weight of the world. Even the clothes he preferred to wear seemed more like armor than an expression of creativity. The trousers cupped his arse. The shirt emphasized his narrow waist. Utilitarian at its finest. Meanwhile, I'd spent all of five minutes this morning tossing on a worn pair of jeans and a black T-shirt that was a few years too old. The fabric stretched tight across my wide shoulders and flirted with my waistline. It should have gone in the bin ages ago, but I'd kept it out of spite, secretly enjoying the way the snug fit made me feel good.

Any enjoyment I might have felt wearing it in Kirill's presence was entirely short-lived. The moment he was sure that Beck and Eren were out of earshot, his gaze turned stony with an emotion I could only classify as *fury*.

I dropped my arms back down to my sides just as he bit out, "Take a seat."

"Kiryusha—"

"Take. A. Seat." Each word left his mouth like a round from a chamber. Hard. Deadly. When I didn't immediately move to obey, he clamped a hand down on the chair that held his jacket and jerked it away from the table. The wooden feet clattered against the tile floor. "Sit," he growled.

"You could at least say please."

Wrong move.

His dark eyes blazed with an inferno that I was embarrassed to say lit me aflame. I loved tender Kirill. I loved the Kirill who'd written me pages upon pages of letters from the other side of the world. But if the last few years had taught me anything, it was that I also loved this version of him, too—the coldhearted soldier whose claws I knew would carve me open while he dragged me kicking and screaming down to the darkest depths of Hell.

Which had to be the only reason I was mad enough to poke the angry beast by adding, "I don't answer to you."

"Oh, but I think you do."

To my surprise, he sidestepped the table. His gait was still agitated—I'd known him for way too long to miss the clipped, angry strides that were usually so smooth and loose-limbed—but the rage in his voice had opted for a different tactic, softening to a dangerous purr that coated my veins like the sweetest poison.

"The first time your father made me watch you, I nearly threw up from the guilt."

I jerked my head to the side just in time to see him disappear behind me. Like a predator stalking its prey, he proved elusive. When I twisted the other way, hoping to catch a glimpse of him, he evaded me once again to stand just out of arm's reach. He had me turned upside down, twisted inside out, my reflexes shoddy from the uncertainty of what he'd do or say next. The rich scent of him, though, filled my nose. Cedarwood with a hint of the sea. I wanted nothing more than to bury my face in his neck and rub his scent all over me.

"It started out innocently enough," Kirill continued in a falsely good-humored murmur, "with you on your back, hands resting on your belly. I thought to myself, *I miss him*. Because I did, Yaroslav. I missed you so fucking much, I thought I would die from the loss of you."

"I missed you, too—"

"I would have done anything to get back to you—so, I did. I became your father's little spy." A cruel smile dripping with self-loathing twisted his lips. "It felt wrong to spy on you when you were so incredibly clueless. Rightfully so, I might add. Why would you think that you were being watched? Your father is a lot of things, but he'd never crossed that line before—not with you or your sister." Gaze shuttering, Kirill passed a hand over his mouth. When he pulled it away, the dark smile curving his lips was gone. "I told myself that invading your privacy was worth whatever pain I might cause you, so long as I actually got to come home in the end. But that was before you started playing with the button on your jeans . . ."

My breath caught in my throat.

"You were insatiable, weren't you?" The tenor of his voice dropped to a husky rumble. "Fucking shameless."

"I thought that I was alone," I uttered hoarsely.

"You weren't."

"Did you watch me?" The question leapt from my tongue before I could wrangle it into submission. There were butterflies swarming in my stomach. Any second now, I was going to pass the fuck out. "When I was . . . When I touched myself, I mean. Did you watch?"

"No."

Disappointment nearly dropped me to my knees.

"I refused to watch you." His midnight-black eyes bored into me with such fierce intensity that I felt lightheaded. "When you touched yourself, I turned the audio off, made sure to focus my attention elsewhere. And when you finished, I made sure to delete every trace of you jacking off from the server, or looking up porn on the internet, or whatever the fuck else you were doing at three in the morning when you thought everyone was asleep."

Porn. On the internet.

The white noise buzzing in my ears was now a thunderous roar. Fuck provoking the beast, I wanted to run away and never, ever look back. He knew. He *knew* that I'd been watching gay porn—everything from docking to frottage to coming hands-free—and I could see it in the dark glimmer of his eyes, in the way he held himself apart from me, that he had kept this secret for years now.

Had he realized, too, that I was hopelessly in love with him?

I opened my mouth to defend myself, to spew some rubbish lie that neither one of us would believe. Only, to my burning shame, nothing came out.

I stumbled backward, fear and panic pummeling me from all angles, but Kirill—he followed, tracking my harried escape across Beck's kitchen, never letting me out of his sight.

"You could have used those midnight hours to murder someone, and I would have gotten rid of the evidence. For you, Yarik. Anything for you. Because I made a vow to protect you, no matter what." His features distorted with an emotion that I wasn't even sure I could properly name—betrayal, anger, resentment. Some horrid blend of all three. "Imagine my surprise," he growled, "when I realized that you couldn't do the same for me."

He pulled something small from his pocket and threw it on the floor. It rolled once, twice, thrice, before skidding to a stop halfway between us. It was compact and made of plastic, its hard shell a deep, dark gray that appeared almost black.

A body camera.

The kind that all of my father's men wore around me.

The kind that *Kirill* wore around me.

It cracked in two beneath the heavy weight of his shoe. "Did it ever occur to you that I'd find out? That I might pull up the feed from the club, the very next day, to delete a private moment that I wouldn't want hand-delivered to your father on a silver platter?"

Oh, *fuck*.

Eyes wide, my heart rabbited so fiercely that I was actually panting.

Kirill wasn't done with me.

In a voice like ice, he ground out, "And there you were, weren't you?"

Something hard and immovable collided with my spine, impeding my getaway. A quick jerk of my chin revealed that I was pressed up against a wall in Beck's lounge. I was bigger than Kirill, stronger, too, if not necessarily faster. There was nothing to stop me from shoving him out of the way and getting out of here.

Only, I'd been anticipating this confrontation, hadn't I? The guilt, the endless shame. I'd felt the first stirrings of each that night when I'd watched him, but in the three days that followed, I'd done nothing but drown in them both.

He was right, of course. In that bathroom, with nothing but a wall and a mirror to keep us apart, I'd thought of only my own desires. I deserved his wrath. For many different reasons, honestly, but mostly because maybe, if he hated me enough, it'd finally get through my stupid, fucking brain that *he didn't want me.*

I couldn't keep living like this—I wouldn't survive it.

We wouldn't survive it.

"Did you watch me?"

At the gravel in his voice, I squeezed my eyes shut. "You already know the answer."

"I want you to *own* it," my best friend growled hotly. "Did you watch me, Yarik?"

Mortification bled into every cell in my body.

"Yes," I whispered, my skin hot with shame.

"Did you touch yourself, thinking of her?"

The laugh that crawled up my throat sounded tragically bitter. "Does it make you feel better to think that? If so, then yeah. Sure did. Fucking made myself come all over my hand thinking of the hot little blonde sucking you off, the one you could barely bring yourself to look at."

He hissed through his teeth. "Careful, now."

"I touched myself thinking of *you!*" I exploded, my hands shaped into tight, trembling fists down at my sides. It was too late to snatch the confession back. Too late to do much of anything but double down and lie in the grave I'd dug myself. "Because that's what I do, Kirill. I dream of you—in bed, with my hand around my aching dick, or at the club, watching your reflection in the mirror, wishing you'd only look at me."

Surprise flashed in his unfathomably dark eyes. "I-I look at you."

"Not the way that I look at you."

"Yarik—"

"Do I disgust you? Is that it?" Somehow, the tables had turned, putting me on the offensive even though I didn't dare move a single muscle. I dragged in shattered breath after shattered breath, staring helplessly at the boy I'd loved for over ten years, with my back still pressed against the wall, entirely at his mercy. "Is it one thing to know your best mate gets off to gay porn but something else entirely to know that he wants all of that with *you*? Because I want that," I said, for the first time in my life not shying away from the truth. "I want you to fuck me, Kiryusha. I want you to make me scream your name, to carve my nails down your spine so that you remember me always, but most of all, I want you to *beg* for me."

"Shut up," he said, but his voice shook with the effort it took to get the words out. His cheeks were stained red with a furious flush. "Stop talking, okay? Just *stop talking*."

"No. If this is the only chance I'll get to tell you how I really feel, then you're just going to have to take it."

His hand found the front of my T-shirt, twining the material around his fist. Maybe so he could hold me in place when he knocked my lights out. Maybe so he could yell at me some more. All I knew was that he watched me the way a tiger might watch an approaching predator from its perch in the jungle, almost bewildered to find another of its ilk encroaching on territory that it had always called home.

Kirill was my home.

Wherever he went, I'd fit myself there beside him even if it meant that I fed on days-old scraps.

"I want you more than I want my next breath." The admission was raw, completely unfiltered. It left me swaying from an overwhelming sense of relief, a burden that I no longer carried alone. "I've wanted you for *years*. And I can tell you that I'm sorry for watching you the other night, but that would be a lie—I'm not sorry. I'm not sorry at all."

Quick, uneven breaths slipped past his lips.

And then glassy, midnight-eyes dropped down to my mouth.

"Every page of my life has you written between the lines. You could walk away right now, and that still wouldn't change how I feel about you." Because I was weak for him, utterly *hopeless*. I always would be. "So, go." I shoved his chest. "Get out of here. If you don't want me, there's the fucking door."

He didn't budge.

If anything, his hand coiled the fabric of my shirt even tighter. Whether he realized it or not, he'd pulled me forward so that I hovered over him. I wanted to place my hands on his hips. I wanted to dig my nails into his skin and mark him forever. But both of those options involved touching him, and I didn't know what to do with the mixed signals he was sending. Swallowing hard, I searched his face, seeking any confirmation that he wanted this—that he wanted *me*.

His color was still high, his pulse pounding almost feverishly in the hollow of his throat. Then his lips parted like he was about to receive a kiss, and he nervously touched his tongue to his bottom lip.

I was fucking *done*.

"Let me taste you, Kiryusha."

As if he was a skittish colt, I lifted my trembling hand slowly, allowing my palm to drift over his cheek without actually touching him. So, so close, but I refused to close that final gap—not until he surrendered or at least gave me permission to take what I wanted. What I'd *always* wanted—him.

"Just once," I begged roughly, "please."

His gaze snapped up to meet mine.

He didn't say no.

He didn't tell me to fuck off.

He didn't do anything besides lift his chin, and that

was really all I needed. With every bit of my heart and soul, I cradled his cheek like he was precious to me, then lowered my head in tiny increments, giving him every chance to pull away, to put a stop to this, once and for all.

Our noses brushed. My thumb grazed his cheekbone in a gentle, careful caress that I'd ached to give him for over a decade, since that night I'd found him by the river, his skin caked in mud. I breathed him in, that scent of cedarwood and the sea that smelled of home, and felt his warm, shaky breath tease my lips with the promise of more.

I'd waited eleven years to make Kirill Volkov mine.

I couldn't wait a second longer.

Letting my eyes flutter shut, I slanted my mouth down over his and—

CHAPTER TWENTY-SIX

KIRILL

H e kissed me.

...To be continued in Kiss of Death

THANK YOU, DARLING

Thank you so much for taking a chance on Yarik & Kirill!

I promise that all hope is not lost, and our boys will get their much deserved HEA in Book 2 of the No Mercy Duet, Kiss of Death. In the QR Code Below, be sure to...

Pre-Order Kiss of Death
Add Kiss of Death to your Goodreads TBR
DM Mia to yell at her (hi, that's me) for that cliffhanger!

I hope that you enjoyed the first part of Yarik & Kirill's story. When I decided to write a childhood best friends to enemies to lovers romance, I knew immediately that I wanted to let those early years of the relationship take center stage however I could. Initially, I only planned for Villain to be a short story (confession: until close to publication, the title for the book in my Word Doc remained "Yarik + Kirill: Short Story") but these two boys . . .

They demanded everything from me.

Soon, one extra chapter became two, and then three became four, and suddenly I'd gone back to write the entirety of Part IV.

Villain still has the feeling of a "prequel" or origin story, but in my heart, it is dedicated to every single one of you who not only love a sweeping romance that spans years, but most especially, it is for every single person who has ever wished for something with their entire being, only for it to always remain just out of grasp.

I see you.

I hope that in these pages, you felt seen, too.

My hope is to get Kiss of Death out in the latter half of 2024, so please stay tuned for lots of book edging until that day comes! My inbox is always open for angry pitchforks (I know, I know, Chapter 15 is rough ::cries::), random hellos, or book recs.

xoxo,

Mia

RUSSIAN GLOSSARY

Otets – Father, formal address
Da – *yeah*
Dvoyurodnyy brat – *cousin (boy)*
Glupyy – *dumb/stupid*
Idi na hui – *fuck yourself*
Idite syuda – *come here*
Konoshno – *of course*
Nyet – *no*
Patsan – *kid*
Ponyal(a) – *I got it*
Pozhaluysta – *please*
Syn – *son*

Turkish Glossary

Kardeş – *brother/friend/pal/buddy*

ACKNOWLEDGMENTS

I can't believe this era of Yarik & Kirill has reached an end, and I am so incredibly grateful—and humbled—by every person who has taken the time to help bring Kiss of Villain out into the world.

To my cover designer, Najla, you and your team have weaved magic with the Villain covers—both the illustrated and model editions. I am forever obsessed with your work. And to my amazing editor, Kathy—I will always hear your voice in my head while I write my little heart out.

To my beta readers, Tiana (@aliterarygoddess) and Maya Jean (@mayajeanwrites), I owe you both a limb, and if not a limb, then at least my endless love. Your kindness, your support—I am just so thankful to both of you, especially when talking me off the ledge!

And to you Darling Reader, a million thank you's. To every bookstagrammer who took a chance on this book and made my jaw drop with your beautiful edits; to those of you creating group chats just to discuss the pure *angst* in these pages; and to every single one of you who took a chance on my words and placed your trust in me—thank you from the bottom of my heart.

You are the reason my dream has come true.

ABOUT THE AUTHOR

Mia Darling lives in a ruined castle and spends her days surrounded by morally grey men vying for her attention... Just kidding.

She lives with her husband and two rambunctious pups who run her life. She loves dragons, things that go bump in the night, and vulnerable anti-heroes who fall in love.

Her M/M Romances are dirty, dangerous, and always end in an HEA. Enemies-to-lovers is her jam, but so is mutual pining. Either way, hold on tight because shit's about to get wild.

♡ Stalk Me, Darling ♡

Join My Newsletter | Instagram | Facebook | TikTok | Goodreads